Raining Down Redemption

BK Rivers

Raining Down Redemption

Copyright © 2016 by BK Rivers.
All rights reserved.
First Print Edition: August 2016

Limitless Publishing, LLC
Kailua, HI 96734
www.limitlesspublishing.com

Formatting: Limitless Publishing

ISBN-13: 978-1-68058-741-8
ISBN-10: 1-68058-741-2

Dedication

For those who believe in second chances…
and in first loves…
this book is for you.

Chapter 1

Jordan

The energy in this arena is electric—it makes the blood in my veins pound to the rhythmic chanting of the awaiting crowd. They scream out, alternating between my name and our latest hit single—the one I wrote for Jemma. I haven't seen her in almost fifteen months. Man, I miss that girl. We take the stage. The fans scream, and lights flash a bright white and rain down scorching heat, making me remember just how hot the Phoenix summers can be. Except it's the middle of January. We run through our set list, and almost two hours later I'm drenched in sweat. My clothes stick to every inch of my body, and now the ride is over.

White Shadow's Recovery Tour is over.

Our PR rep suggested the title since I finally chose to stay clean twenty months ago, and in truth, the band needed something to promote change. It's been a bumpy road, but it feels incredible. I can't believe after almost eight years I've completed

1

months of shows without drugs or alcohol. That had never happened before I met Jemma.

Backstage, all six of us can't contain our smiles as we hug and slap shoulders. A successful concert will do that to you—bring out the most girlish feelings in the manliest of men. I've put these guys, my friends, through hell over the years, but fences have been mended with this tour, and we're stronger than ever.

"Food?" Carson, our keyboardist, suggests. It's tradition now that I'm clean. We find an all-night diner, talk about the show, and stuff our bellies. Tonight is no exception. Except we're back home in Phoenix, and there's only one place we all want to go since we haven't been in years: Eggceptional. Best pancakes in the state of Arizona. We jump in the van and take off toward the hole-in-the-wall diner on Fifteenth, not even stopping to discuss the matter.

The six of us spill out of the van and trudge through the almost empty parking lot. The diner looks the same, tucked into the corner of an old black-and-white brick building with the 1950s neon diner waitress flashing above the entrance. Once inside, the air is thick with old grease and the salty scent of bacon, and I feel at home. The guys and I used to come here throughout high school and up until we scored our record deal.

We slide into a large booth near the back and study the menu, even though I'm pretty sure we all know what we want. You come here three times a week for three years and you get to know the menu fairly intimately.

"Yep, buttermilk pancakes and the Rocky Mountain Scramble are calling my name," Drake says as he rubs his belly. "What are you all having?"

The guys mumble their responses as Grant glances up and blows out a low whistle.

"Look at those legs," he says, his eyes nearly popping out of his skull. "Damn, I'd like to—" The waitress turns, and my brain stutters, like it has trouble keeping pace with my racing heart. "Holy shit, is that Reggie?" Grant clears his throat, glancing to me. "Shit, man. I didn't know. Sorry."

I wave him off and inhale, the huge gulp of air catching in my throat. "It's fine, bro." I cough, pounding a fist to my chest. "We haven't seen each other since graduation."

"You two were inseparable, though."

"That was a long time ago." The years since high school have been really good to her; she's filled out, looking more like a woman than a teenager. When she glances over to our table, she stops dead in her tracks. Her smile fades, eyes widen, and her fingers grip the pitcher of water she's holding. Her long brown hair is tied at the base of her neck, and her cheeks carry a hint of rose pink. And her lips, I can still remember how they feel—how they taste. Slowly she shakes her head side to side like she's chasing away a memory. Her slender hand tucks a stray hair behind her ear and lingers on her jaw as she makes her way to our table.

The simple gesture, so familiar, shakes me to my core, and a memory hits me where I'm eighteen and sitting with Reggie behind the football field

3

bleachers. We're holding hands and talking about the future. Mine hopefully included a record deal; hers was working towards a classroom of her own. Teaching was her passion; music was mine. My hands grip the fabric of her jeans at her hips as I pull her between my legs. She practically purrs at my touch, and all coherent thought is lost when our lips crush together. She tastes like spearmint and summer heat, and when her hands trail down my arms to stop at the top of my thighs, I declare it time to head back to my place. My girl is too good to take behind the football field.

Nine years ago, it was like Reggie was built just for me—we fit together perfectly—like two puzzle pieces coming together. It killed me when she walked away from me shortly after graduation. Looking back now, I understand why she did, and I'm glad for it. It wouldn't have been fair to her, having me gone, high, and screwing any girl who came my way. Sometimes I wonder how I'm still alive after all the shit I've done.

"How have you all been?" I close my eyes at the lilt of her soft voice. She addresses all of us, looking at everyone but me. The air in my chest catches. Damn, I didn't expect it to still hurt so much.

"Reggie! Holy shit, girl, you look amazing," Grant says, wearing the oversized, cheesy grin he uses when he gets his flirt on. I kick him under the table, narrowing my eyes. Okay, maybe I'm not exactly good with anyone but me hitting on her. Reggie's cheeks flush from Grant's compliment as she asks to take our order. When her eyes finally land on me, she swallows slowly and taps her pen on the green order slip.

"How are you?" I ask, before giving her my order. It feels strange to see her again, especially here at Eggceptional. We used to come here when we were dating—the whole high school frequented this place. She and I sat in this very booth and, since it's tucked so far in the back, my fingers got a little frisky more than once under the table.

"I'm good," she says, her voice cracking slightly. "Do you know what you want?" Her dark chocolate hair slips back from behind her ear, and her slender fingers tuck it back again. Her eyes wander while I study her, but I'm interrupted by an elbow in my side from Jeremy.

"Dude, you're bordering on creepy," he whispers, reminding me to place my order.

As she walks away, a pang of guilt—maybe fondness—tugs at me as though there's an invisible string attached to us, and she's tugging on it. She makes herself scarce after our food is delivered, making that string pull tighter. The guys and I discuss our break and make plans to book the recording studio in L.A. in a couple weeks. After we've all eaten until we're sufficiently stuffed, I decide to wait and grab a cab later so the guys can be on their way. I want to hang out longer and talk to Reggie. It's hard for me to comprehend, but I've missed her. I want to get to know her again.

Jeremy slides out from beside me, taking the seat across the table. He folds his arms over the hard surface and stares directly at me. "What are you doing here, cowboy?" He taps his long fingers on the creases of his elbows, studying me like an ant

5

under a magnifying glass.

"I've missed her," I say with a shrug of my shoulders, then scoot against the wall and drape my arms over the back of the booth. Jeremy sighs, rubs his bearded face with his hands, and echoes my posture in the booth.

"Have you missed her for nine years or just since you saw her here an hour ago?"

"What's the difference?" I ask, scanning the floor for her petite frame.

"You can't march up to someone you haven't seen in years and say, 'Hey, I've missed you. Let's go shag in my hotel room.'"

"Shag? Who says that?" A laugh is bubbling in my chest, but Reggie rounds the corner with a pitcher of water, and I swallow it back. I hold up my plastic cup, and she dips her head as if she was already on her way to refill our drinks. Her short black skirt sways with her hips, showing off her toned, olive-skinned legs. Everything about her still makes my body react like it did when I was seventeen.

"You sure you don't want anything stronger than a water?" she asks as the ice clinks from the pitcher into my cup, sending droplets of water onto the table. She refills Jeremy's cup and sits down next to him. A shot of jealous heat rushes to my chest.

"Honey, I gave that shit up almost two years ago."

Her eyes widen in surprise, and a small smile twitches on her rosy lips. Jeremy turns in his seat, resting both arms on the table, and it brings me back to all the times the guys and I hung out with Reggie in high school. Of course there were a few other girls at times, but mostly it was just me, Reggie, and the guys.

"That's really great, Jordan," she says. Her eyes dip to her fidgeting fingers, her long lashes feathering across the apples of her cheeks. "I heard you were giving sobriety a shot."

A smile dances across my lips—she's been keeping tabs on me. "You following up on me, Reggie-bug?" Her back stiffens and her cheeks flush with heat. When I discovered that her middle name was the Spanish word for ladybug, I started calling her Reggie-bug. Sometimes just Bug when the situation fit.

"Please don't call me that," she whispers. Something in the pained way she's looking at me makes that invisible string constrict around my lungs. I've lost my breath at the beauty seated across from me. Her brown eyes have aged; there's a depth to them that wasn't there when we were younger. Suddenly I want to take her in my arms, hold her, and wipe away the sadness I see there.

"So…" Jeremy breaks in. "You work here, huh?"

Her lips turn up in an easy smile, pulling that searing heat of jealousy from me once again. She can smile for him but not me?

She nods and says, "Yep. Almost four years now. How about you guys, what are you doing here?"

We talk for some time about our tour closing and how we're taking a four-month break to record some new songs. The entire conversation I let Jeremy control the flow while I watch Reggie and take in the subtle changes that have settled over her through the years. Her smile has widened, giving her an even more loveable quality, and new creases around her eyes make me wonder about her life, what she's been doing and with whom. Is she married? Does she have kids? For my sake, I hope not on both accounts. I plan to spend a lot of time with her over the next four months.

Reggie drums her fingers on the table before standing. "Break's over. I've got to get back to it." She shrugs, appearing anxious to step away from us.

"It was good catching up," Jeremy says as he clasps his hands together behind his head. "You look good, Reggie. Real good."

"Thanks, Jeremy. You do too."

I'm not ready to say goodbye, not by a long shot. As she walks away, I motion to Jeremy to wait for me. I slide out of the booth and jog to catch her before she slips into the kitchen.

"Reggie, wait up." She stops mid-stride, cradles the empty pitcher in one arm, and rests her free hand on her hip.

"I really have to get back to work."

"I know," I say, maybe a little too fast. A part of me fears losing her once again and, thinking for a moment it's even a possibility, it creates a pit in my stomach, causing even my fingers to ache. "Go out with me," I blurt, filling my cheeks with an unfamiliar rush of heat. Jordan Capshaw doesn't get nervous—I play concerts for thousands of fans.

"Excuse me?" The pitcher slips from the crook of her elbow, but she catches it before it crashes to the ground. "Jordan, I don't think that's a good idea."

"Come on." My hands ball into fists at my sides. *Please don't turn me down.*

"Listen, we had a good run in high school," she says, looking everywhere but at me. "Let's just be happy to have bumped into each other and move on. Can you do that for me, Jordan?" Her brown eyes grow darker as she blinks away the tears gathering along her lower lids. "Please leave." She turns quickly and disappears behind the hammered steel door to the kitchen.

Chapter 2

Reggie

"You look like you've seen a ghost," Rico says as he flips a series of greasy burgers on the grill. "Everything okay?"

I set the empty pitcher on the stainless steel counter and take several deep breaths to try to clear my head. I fall back against the kitchen wall, wrapping my arms around my waist, unable to stop the unwanted tears. They're like cascading waterfalls staining my cheeks and tumbling to the sunset-orange Saltillo tiles at my feet. Rico tucks his grease-smeared spatula into the pocket of his stained apron and wraps his doughy arms around me in a warm hug. He stands only a couple inches over me and outweighs me by at least a hundred pounds, but his gentle hug feels warm and comforting.

When my tears have stopped falling, and after Rico retrieves the burgers from the grill before they burn, I pull a paper towel from the wall and clean up my face.

"Thanks, Rico," I say, hugging him from behind. "I needed that."

"Anytime, girl." He plates the burgers and sends me on my way. I half expect to see Jordan standing where I left him, but despite how persistent I know he can be, he's nowhere to be seen. I release the breath I was holding, paste on a phony smile, and finish my shift.

***

It's after 2 a.m. when I cross the threshold to my apartment and, just as it is every night I work late, Stacey is huddled under her fuchsia blanket watching *SNL* reruns. The cozy blanket falls to her feet when she stands, stretching her arms over her head.

"Hey," she begins sleepily. Her brows knit together when she takes in my frazzled appearance. "Oh, hon, what's wrong?"

Plopping down on the couch, I pull a pillow to my chest and hug it tightly. When I woke up this morning, never in a million years did I expect to run into Jordan Capshaw while working my shift. I mean, I guess it was always possible, but in the four years I've worked at Eggceptional, never once has he set foot inside. And why, oh why did he have to look so good? Everything about him has broadened since high school—his shoulders, his easy smile, his chest. Man, he looked so good. He always kept his face smooth when we were together, and I couldn't help noticing the thick scruff lining his cheeks and how it made me want to run my fingers over it.

I groan into the pillow, trying my best to work out the confusion and nerves zipping through me.

"Is Micah asleep?" I ask, hoping he sure better be.

Stacey nods, lays her arm over my shoulder, and pulls me close. I'm so lucky to have a friend like her; I don't know what I would have done without her.

Melting into her embrace, I sigh heavily. "I saw him tonight. He came into the diner."

Stacey's arm falls from my shoulder, and she sits upright. "Who, Reg?"

"Jordan."

Her jaw moves side to side while she processes the information. "Jordan, *Jordan*? As in…"

"Yep. That Jordan."

She falls against the back of the couch, and I follow, relaxing into the plush microsuede. For a long while we sit in silence, and I think maybe she's fallen asleep. When I finally glance at her she's staring at the ceiling, twisting her lips to the side in concentration.

"So, did you guys talk? Or was it just a passing glance?"

I proceed to run through the night and our conversation, right down to when he asked me out. A cheesy grin works its way onto Stacey's lips, and when she turns to me she scrunches her eyes closed and bursts into laughter. Okay, I was totally not expecting that. Maybe a groan or a sarcastic "yeah right," but a laugh? Is it really that funny?

"You said no, right?" She flips around on the

couch so we're facing each other, and I'm thrust back into high school when we'd have sleepovers and stay up all night talking about boys. Or in my case, Jordan.

"Of course I said no. What kind of girl do you take me for?" I slap her thigh and lean forward until my face falls into the pillow on my lap. "But, Stace, he looked so good."

"The guy is a loser, despite being a rock star." Stacey hasn't always felt this way about Jordan and, in a way, I suppose it's deserved. When his band started touring, it was obvious the fame and money allowed him whatever he wanted, and what he wanted was alcohol and drugs. I'm not sure what made him want to get clean, but I'm impressed and proud of him if he's telling the truth. He deserves more than a life full of regrets.

"He's sober now," I say, trying to drive the point home that he's really not a loser. "And he really, *really* looks good."

Stacey rolls her eyes and swipes my pillow. "We've established that he looks so good you'd like to lick an ice cream sundae off his chest. But come on. How long has it been since you last saw him?"

Not counting the one and only concert I went to four years ago, I haven't seen him since high school graduation, nine years ago, when I urged him to go live his dream. We were eighteen, and his aspirations were so big even the gymnasium couldn't contain them. He and the guys wanted a life I didn't, and I still don't. So when we parted ways it broke my heart, even though I'm the one who pushed him into going after what he wanted most. My plans, however, took a left turn, and now I'm working two jobs and living with my best friend and haven't dated since. I'm the picture of what every twenty-six-year-old woman should be. *Yeah right*.

Shaking myself out of my self-induced pity party, I say, "Whatever. The point is he looks fine, and only tonight did I realize how pathetic I am."

Stacey hits me square in the face with the pillow, and my head jerks back against the cushions.

"What the hell?"

"Quit playing the 'poor me' card. You're smoking hot, a hard worker, and the best mom I know. I'm sure Jordan left Eggceptional thinking of nothing but you." Stacey's little pep talk makes my cheeks flush, and we both giggle until I can't keep my eyes open any longer. Raising a kid and working two jobs isn't for the weary; add to that my average of four hours of sleep a night and I'm wiped.

As I lie in bed, thoughts of me and Jordan in high school flash in my head like a movie. Sophomore year, while I was searching through my locker for a notebook, he came up from behind me, all limbs and smiles. I was still fairly new to the school, as my family had moved to Phoenix a couple months prior. When he asked me what I was looking for, I sighed and described the notebook I needed. He then reached to the top shelf and pulled it out. I wanted to die of embarrassment, but instead I melted in the way his light brown eyes stared at me like there was no one else around.

We were inseparable after that. School dances,

dates every Friday night, and making out behind the football bleachers.

Heat blossoms on my chest as I recall our first kiss and how our teeth collided and we both laughed. But then his tongue ran across my bottom lip, and I just about died. I could've bet I'd burst into flames from the sheer heat raging through my body. Of course, we got better at kissing later on. A whole lot better.

Closing my eyes now only adds fuel to the desire to know if he still kisses the same. If his lips are still as soft as they used to be, or if after almost nine years he's gained more skills in that department. What would his scruffy beard feel like against my lips? Or trailing down my…okay, this is not going to help me sleep. Not one bit.

I'm hit with a heavy dose of reality as Micah stumbles into my room, rubbing the sleep from his big brown eyes. He crawls into bed with me, nuzzles his head under my chin, and promptly falls asleep.

That right there will snuff out any Jordan-inspired fantasies.

Chapter 3

Jordan

I've been back in Phoenix for four days now, staying at a hotel with Jeremy. Which is fine if you're looking for someone to nag you about keeping your room clean. He's a freak when it comes to cleanliness. It's great on the bus, but when we're supposed to be taking some time to relax before we start recording again, it's like a splinter in the fleshy part of your palm—annoying.

Not only is he a clean freak, but he's also really pushing for me to reconcile with my parents. Whenever we come back to town, he's always urging me to call them or at the very least send a freaking postcard to let them know I'm in town. I mean, I know they listen to the radio, and they know the name of my band. I'm sure they're very aware when I'm in Phoenix. They could reach out if they wanted to see me too.

He's convinced that, because we're here for four months, I should really try to make it work with them. It's not like I didn't try when we first went on the road, but all I got from my old man was disappointment and bitterness. Then he had the nerve to tell me what a screw up I've always been. I got pissed, he got even more pissed, and now after everything I haven't spoken to him or Mom in nine years. I imagine if I were to call out of the blue, one of them would keel over, and then I'd have a funeral to go to. Not that I would go, necessarily.

None of that has anything to do with the fact that I'm pacing the floor of the hotel room, cell phone in hand, finger hovering over the Home contact. I really have no freaking clue as to why I'm even considering calling them. Or why when I bring the phone up to my ear it's ringing.

Shit. Did I just dial them?

"Hello?" My mother's voice hits me like a semi, and I collapse on the end of the bed. She sounds older, tired. "Hello?"

Shit. I haven't said anything. I take a deep breath when I hear my father in the background asking her who is on the line. She answers, saying there's no one there. A scratching noise vibrates in my ear, and then my hand grips the phone as my father gets on the phone.

"Whoever the hell you are better stop calling at this time of night," he says as I glance at the clock on the nightstand. Shit. It's after nine, and my parents always said it was rude to call after eight.

I take a deep breath, close my eyes, and say, "Hey, Dad. It's me."

Silence.

Followed by more silence.

I pull the phone away from my ear to check if I somehow dropped the call, but it seems we're still connected. "Hello?" I say as a knot forms in my stomach, and my heart begins to pound out an unsteady rhythm.

"You have some nerve calling us at this time of night," he growls. "Scaring your mother like that." Mom gasps in the background and then says my name, and damn, a tear slips down my cheek. I swipe away the unwanted moisture beading on my cheek and begin to apologize for calling at this hour, but I don't have a chance—my father cuts off the words forming on my lips.

"You're a piece of work, you know? After nine years of pissing yourself away, and now you think you can call us to come bail you out of the mess you've created?"

"Dad, I—"

"Not to mention all the times we've had reporters and those damn paparazzi show up on our doorstep. Never once did you think of what this would do to your mother. You're a selfish son of a—"

I hang up the phone before he finishes, and I'm seething. I throw the phone on the bed, feeling nowhere near satisfied. The familiar clench in my stomach returns, the one that beckons me to just down one shot, or do a line of blow. I thought I could handle being sober, I thought the urges were gone. But my addiction is so hungry I can feel my body tensing and calling for the release I'm craving.

I step over to the mini fridge and take stock of the sample-size bottles of alcohol sitting in a neat line on one of the shelves and lick my lips. Some of my best friends are sitting there waiting for me: Jack, José, and Captain Morgan. I pull a bottle of Jack from the fridge, hold the chilled glass in my hand, and take several deep breaths.

Shit.

I can't call Jeremy because he's home with his parents for the night, and the clinic in Warner is closed for the night; though I probably could call one of the counselors. My fist grips the bottle harder, and I grab my phone off the bed and dial the only other person who has ever been able to talk me down from this ugly place.

"Hello? Jordan?" I release the breath I was holding at the sound of her voice. It's been a long time since we've spoken, and I've missed her.

"Hey," I sigh, and then squeeze the small bottle of Jack even tighter. Maybe if I keep squeezing, it will burst in my hand and solve the problem for me.

"Are you okay?" Jemma's voice is riddled with nervousness, and she has every right to be. I haven't spoken to her in a few months, and she's probably thinking I'm drunk dialing. She wouldn't be too far from the truth.

I shake my head, close my eyes, and let the tears fall freely. God, I'm a mess, and I'm so close to screwing everything up again.

"I don't think I am," I admit, and slip down to the floor at the foot of the bed. I pull my knees to my chest and lay my head on my arms.

"What can I do? Jordan, tell me how to help you."

"I've got a travel-size bottle of Jack Daniels in

19

my hand, and there are several others in this hotel fridge."

She gasps on the other end and then breathes out calmly. "Have you opened the bottle?"

I shake my head and then realize she can't see me. "No. But I want to. So bad."

"Why, Jordan? Why do you want to drink?"

"I don't want to talk about it. I want to hear how you're doing. How's Vic?"

I can practically hear the smile that fills her face as she tells me all about how they went to Seattle to get married and how they're going to have a baby in April. I tell her how happy I am for her and Vic, but inside, pieces of my heart crumble just a little bit. It doesn't seem all that long ago I thought I was in love with Jemma. But in reality, I think it was only the idea that someone *could* love me. That maybe *I'm* capable of loving someone, and I *want* to love someone.

"Jordan, I think you should find a counselor in Phoenix to talk to," she says quietly. "You can call me any time you need to; I'll always be here for you. I just think you need someone nearby as well."

Her words ring true and I realize she's right. Even though I thought I could handle my addiction on my own, I wasn't able to without the help from the rehab clinic in Warner and the counselors there.

"Thanks, Jemma. I'll call someone first thing in the morning."

"Sure," she says. "Jordan, will you do something for me?"

"Anything," I answer, knowing I truly would.

"Open all of those bottles and pour them down

the drain."

We share a nervous laugh, and she remains on the line while I pour every last drop of the seven bottles of alcohol down the drain. When I hang up, I pull up the Internet browser on my phone and search for drug addiction counselors in Phoenix. This is one call that may just save my life.

Chapter 4

Reggie

This is my Saturday to bring Micah to Mom and Dad's house so they can spend time with him—and berate me. I'm not sure why I keep putting up with their criticism other than the fact that Micah should spend time with his grandparents and, as much as I can't stand their constant questions, it gives me a little reprieve from parenting.

We moved to Phoenix when I was fifteen because my dad got a new job working as a school principal. Thank goodness it wasn't in the district where I went to high school, otherwise I don't think I would've been able to get away with half the stuff I used to do. Last year he decided to retire, and he and Mom moved up north to Flagstaff so they could enjoy the weather from all four seasons. Personally, I can't stand the snow, and my little Toyota Corolla isn't equipped for icy roads. Thankfully, Flagstaff hasn't seen any snow for two weeks, which is somewhat abnormal for January.

Hefting two small suitcases into the trunk, I check that Micah is safely buckled in the backseat and hug Stacey goodbye. We pull away from the apartment complex, and I hear the familiar music of Micah's iPad and the games he likes to play on the drive.

It's roughly a three-hour drive from Phoenix to Flagstaff, and I feel guilty that I have the radio playing and Micah is on his iPad the whole drive, but at least he doesn't ask me if we're there yet every five minutes.

My parents' house is a little brown A-frame that sits on the edge of a wooded hill, their nearest neighbor about three hundred feet away. They exchanged the close-knit neighborhood of our Phoenix home for the country life and are very content. Mom gardens and raises chickens; Dad works in the shop at the rear of the property. Puffy white smoke rises from the stone chimney, and Mom meets us at the red front door when we pull up and park. Her cheeks are flushed, and her hair is neatly styled in a perfect black bob that accentuates her cheekbones.

Micah leaps out of the car, iPad forgotten, and runs to my mom, who kneels down and pulls him into a warm embrace. A sad sigh is pulled from my chest when remembering what those embraces used to feel like. I haven't been on the receiving end of one of her genuine hugs since I told her I was pregnant with Micah. Not that I can really blame her. I was young and unmarried, and the father was out of the picture. But the lack of affection still stings, though I'm glad she freely gives it to Micah.

"Sweetheart, I was beginning to think you had forgotten us," she says as she pats Micah's head and gently pushes him inside the house.

"Of course I didn't forget, Mom. I had to stop a couple times for Micah to use the bathroom." And to grab something made of chocolate for me, but I don't tell her that. Though sometimes I think she's psychic or can read minds because she says, "You really should lay off the sweets, dear," as her finger brushes of a stray bit of candy bar from the corner of my lip. Damn chocolate. You have to go and betray me too?

"So what do you guys have planned for us this weekend?" I ask, steering the conversation away from my addiction to sweets.

"Oh, the usual." Mom sweeps us inside, calls for Dad to grab our suitcases, and ushers Micah and me into the spare bedroom at the top of the stairs. They bought this house from another retired couple who decided they wanted to cash in their equity for a large RV and travel the states. In some regard, I guess I could see the allure of traveling wherever you want, but I'm happy in Phoenix. I'm happy staying in one place and putting down roots.

Micah finds the heavy winter jacket Mom keeps for him in the closet, shoves on a pair of thick gloves, and runs down the stairs and out the backdoor before I have time to take a breath. He loves Mom's chickens and, more often than not, I need only look in the coop and he's got one or two of them on his lap, petting them and talking sweetly.

That boy really needs a dog.

"Where do you want these?" Dad asks from the bedroom door. He's brought up both suitcases and no doubt is ready to return to his news show or maybe his woodshop. I point to the same corner by the closet where I have him place them every time we come to visit. He nods, lifts them with a grunt, and places them where I pointed.

"Thanks, Dad." He nods again and practically races out of the room. I plop on one of the two twin beds in the room and lie flat on my back. I never thought I'd end up being a single mom, working two jobs just to make ends meet. But then again, I wouldn't trade a minute with Micah. He's a bright light in my life that keeps me going on tough days and makes me smile with his crazy antics.

After dinner, I help Mom clean up the kitchen while Dad and Micah play a game of *Sorry!* I love the way my little boy laughs, the sound so innocent it melts my heart. The four of us play another round when the kitchen is clean, and then I go through our bedtime routine and bring Micah upstairs to put him to bed.

"I love coming to see Grammy and Gramps," he says with a drowsy smile. "Why can't we come every weekend?"

"You know why," I say, kissing his little button nose. "I have to work and only have one weekend off a month."

"Julietta pecked my finger today." Mom's head hen is known to be a little territorial.

"Oh yeah? Did it hurt?"

He shakes his head and stares up at me with wide, brown eyes. "I was brave, like a superhero.

25

They don't cry when a chicken pecks their finger."

I pinch his cheek and smile at his logic. "No, I suppose they wouldn't cry. I love you, my sweet little boy. I'll see you in the morning, okay?" He nods and his lids lower, his long lashes fanning across his pink cheeks. Man, I love this boy.

I find Mom and Dad sitting on the couch sipping their chamomile tea and notice the room is silent except for the ticking of the clock hanging on the wall. Before I have time to turn around and escape their inquisition, Dad calls for me to join them. I swallow the lump in my throat and prepare myself for whatever lecture they have in store for me this time.

I leap onto the overstuffed armchair like a teenager, and fold my legs under me. Almost in unison, both my parents take another sip of tea and set it back on matching end tables they bought at Costco.

Dad clears his throat and glances at Mom, raising his eyes at her. He's never the one to do the talking—it's always her and very little me.

"We think it's time you and Micah move up here," she says point blank. We've had this discussion many times, and I always tell her the same thing: I'm happy where I am and don't want to move or take Micah away from the school he's in. As I open my mouth to argue my point like I always do, she waves a hand, dismissing me.

"We've found a nice place near an elementary school that we've put a deposit down to hold it. You can start moving in as soon as Monday, and Micah can start school as well. You can go and pack up your apartment tomorrow and start bringing stuff up right away. Micah can stay with us until you get settled, that way he can get acquainted with Mrs. Richardson, his teacher, and meet some friends."

My jaw drops. They did what?

"Micah will just love Mrs. Richardson, and she says there are a couple boys who she thinks will be great friends for our boy." Mom's smile is stretched so wide it makes her eyes look cat-like.

"Mom," I say with a groan. "You can't just go around placing a deposit on an apartment for Micah and me. We've been through this. I like living in Phoenix and so does Micah."

She breaks her smile, trading it in for a sardonic laugh. "Honey, it's a *house*, not an apartment. And you can't live with Stacey forever." She thinks because it's a house that I'll concede to moving?

"I don't care if it's a freaking mansion, Mom. I'm not ripping Micah out of school halfway through the year and moving him away from all his current friends."

"You need to think about what's best for Micah," Mom says through clenched teeth. "He needs a father figure in his life, and you're sure not going to get it from Micah's father. I see how much he enjoys spending time with your dad; he needs that."

"Not once have you supported my decisions since I told you I was pregnant. I'm tired of you treating me like I'm still a child whom you can order around. Micah and I are not moving, end of discussion."

This time, Mom full-on laughs, and it's like a

knife stabbing into my stomach over and over. My hands ball into fists while my arms fold over my chest. I'm pissed she thinks she has the right to do any of this, to expect this from me. Does she not realize I have a responsibility to Stacey for half the rent or how moving may affect Micah?

"Your decisions have always been poor. Take Micah's father for example—what a deadbeat he's turned out to be. We should never have allowed the two of you to date. To think he shares his DNA with—"

"I've had enough. You have no right to ask this of me. I've said it before—I'm not moving." I stand up and head for the stairs. "I'm taking Micah home right now, and I don't want to have this discussion ever again." Taking the stairs two at a time doesn't get me to the room fast enough. My heart is pounding, chest heaving, and I'm on the verge of breaking down. But I won't do that here. I can't let her know how much her words have hurt me. Quietly, I drag the suitcases out of the room and out the front door. I load them up and then storm back up the stairs and pull Micah into my arms.

"Hey, sleepyhead, we're going back home," I whisper against his soft hair. He nods and tucks his head into my shoulder. Carefully, I make my way back downstairs, through the door, and then buckle him securely in the backseat and walk around to the driver's side.

"Yet another poor decision on your part," Mom snaps from the doorway. "Always making stupid mistakes."

"Well, at least this is one mistake I won't make

again," I say, opening the car door. "If you want to see your grandson next month, I would suggest not ruining the trip by trying to plan out my life for me." With that I climb inside my car, shut the door, and start the engine. I've never spoken to my parents that way, and it felt surprisingly good. Really good. For too long I've let my mom try to dictate how I live my life. Well, from now on I deserve better.

Chapter 5

Jordan

Our week in the hotel will be up tomorrow, which means one of two things. One, I continue to pay astronomical amounts of money each week for the remaining four months we're here, or two, I look for a condo to lease. Jeremy steps through the hotel door without knocking—it should probably bother me, but ever since I called him all those months ago practically begging him to talk the guys into taking me back, he's been my shadow. I don't know if he's waiting for me to slip up or if he's only trying to be a good friend. Either way, it feels good knowing he has my back.

"Looking good, JD," I say. He smiles, runs his hand over his cleanly shaved jaw, and pulls a chair out from the small table and sits down. On tour, most of us sport some degree of the five o'clock shadow, and while mine has been more beard-like as of late, it always takes me a bit to get used to baby-faced Jeremy Dixon.

"You're just jealous I still look like I'm eighteen, despite being twenty-six. Too bad your ugly old mug keeps looking older." I'm older than him by two months and could pass for eighteen if I tried. Not that I have any reason to.

"I think it's time to find a short-term lease." I scrub my hands through my hair, waiting for Jeremy's response. "Maybe a two-bedroom?" Jeremy's eyes lift in my direction. I'm guessing he wasn't expecting me to invite him to live with me.

"Yeah." He shrugs. "Makes sense. When should we start looking?"

I'm not sure why I was so afraid he'd laugh at me or tell me I'm crazy for wanting to lease a condo, but it feels like a hundred pounds has just fallen from my shoulders now that he's agreed. At least he'll be around to keep an eye on me, and that's a comfort.

"I've already called a leasing agency and have an appointment this morning to go see a couple places. You ready to go?" Jeremy nods, and we head out.

The agency is on the third floor of a brick building in downtown Phoenix. The view overlooks a rooftop patio across the street. Jeremy and I sit in beige leather chairs in the waiting area in front of a curvaceous blond—Reagan—with bright red lips and a messy bun on the top of her head. Every so often she glances over the top of her computer screen and shoots us a squinty grin. After the third glance, I meet her up at her desk and rest my arms across the counter.

"I hate to be impatient, Reagan, but I'm kind of on a deadline. Do you know how much longer it

31

will be?" Her red lips turn down in a pout as she picks up her phone. At the same time, the opaque, sky blue door swings open and Reggie steps out. She glances at Reagan and then me, and her cheeks flush.

"What are you doing here?" Reggie asks as her fingers absentmindedly linger on her jaw, before her hand clasps over my elbow as she pulls me back to Jeremy. "Are you both stalking me?" she asks in a whisper.

"What the hell, Jordan? Did you know she worked here?" Jeremy asks. His face pinches while he rubs the bridge of his nose.

Laughing at the way Reggie and Jeremy are wearing matching expressions probably wasn't the best idea since it earned me a slap on the shoulder from Reggie and a punch in the ribs from Jeremy.

"I had no idea Reggie worked here. The reviews for the agency were the best, so I called and made the appointment." Reggie folds her arms across her chest, looking unimpressed. "I'm serious, I really didn't know."

"Whatever, dude. Let's just get this over with," Jeremy says, shaking his head and gritting his teeth.

We follow Reggie through the door and back into her small office. Jeremy and I sit at two chairs in front of a sleek, glass-topped desk. Reggie takes her seat, pulls out some paperwork, spreads it out before us, and explains what each form is and how it protects our rights as tenants and clients of the agency. Once we've signed at the necessary places, her attention is what's on the computer screen.

Seeing her the other day at Eggceptional looking

so good in that short skirt has nothing on the way she looks today. Her hair is down in long waves that cascade down her back; red slacks hug her hips just right, and the black-and-white striped, cap-sleeved shirt shows off her curves. The small office is fairly dull in décor but what catches my attention is the lack of personal photos anywhere. That, and the lack of a ring on her left hand.

"It's more difficult finding short-term leases in the winter," she says, drawing me back to the subject at hand. "With all the winter visitors here, most of the rentals are already gone."

"My budget is pretty flexible," I add, and then flinch when her eyes close and then flutter open. "What I mean is I can afford pretty much anything." Shit. Insert foot into mouth now. However, a flash of something playful flashes over her face, and I wonder if she's just issued some sort of challenge.

"Is that so?" she says, a smile dancing on her rosy lips. "Well, this may just make my month."

Jeremy reaches across the desk and lays his hand on Reggie's wrist. Her head snaps around, and her eyes dart down at his hand before glancing at me.

"I'm in this lease too, and I have no intention of paying out my ass for a place to live for four months. So please find us something within reason." Jeremy releases Reggie's arm and sits back in his chair.

"I'll see what I can come up with," she says in an almost whisper.

Jeremy and I exchange silent threats, him telling me to behave, me telling him to keep his bear claws off my girl. After almost ten minutes of our unspoken warnings, Reggie excuses herself from the office.

"What are we really doing here?" Jeremy asks, his face turning an odd shade of radish.

"I was dead serious, dude. I had no clue she worked here."

"You're lying. And quit with the 'I have enough money to buy whatever I want' attitude."

I really hadn't meant for it to come out like that. Something about seeing Reggie again has me all agitated, causing the words in my head to twist into blurts of nothingness.

Before I can respond, Reggie glides through the door, and suddenly I'm on my feet and two sets of eyes stare blankly at me. Heat flames through my neck and as I try to cover up my strange behavior with a cough, the stares don't go away. Instead, Reggie hands me a small stack of papers, giving me the details of the condos she's found for us to take a look at.

"This is all the pertinent data on the condos we're going to go see," she says as she gathers her purse and fishes out her car keys. She grimaces and then glances back to me and Jeremy.

"I hate to do this, but it's company policy for us to take a photocopy of your driver's licenses and keep them in the file." Jeremy and I pull out our wallets and hand her our licenses. "Everything here is confidential and it should go without saying, but your personal information will be held in strict confidence."

"Then why do you need the copies?" I ask, a little apprehensive to hand over my ID. I trust

Reggie explicitly, but the people she works with, not so much.

"It's for our own safety," she says with a shrug before snatching the cards from our hands and disappearing out the door, only to return a few moments later and return our licenses. "Are you ready?" We follow her to the elevator and into the parking garage under the building. Her car is a silver Toyota Corolla, nothing fancy, and it smells clean with a hint of vanilla and spice, just like her. Jeremy takes the front passenger seat, and I climb into the back and sit in the center. Beside me is an iPad, and I must be part cat because curiosity is getting the better of me.

I press the button on the bottom and see a picture of Reggie and her friend I recognize from high school posing in front of the camera wearing nearly identical duck lips and cross-eyed looks. She looks happy and seeing this comforts me, even if it's just a small amount. Deciding not to pry any more, I press the power button and lay the iPad on the center console between Reggie and Jeremy.

"You left your iPad in the backseat," I say before sitting against the back of the seat and stretching my arms out to the side.

Chapter 6

Reggie

I almost slammed on the brakes in the middle of the busy downtown streets when Jordan handed up Micah's iPad. Not once did I consider something of Micah's may be in the car. I mean, he often leaves little toys or papers from school in the backseat. A wave of nausea surges through me while I silently pray there is no other evidence of my son in the backseat with Jordan. A part of me is dying to look at the iPad's wallpaper on the screen to see if there is one of the hundreds of pictures of me and Micah together. What if he looked at the screen?

All I can do is remind myself to breathe. Breathe and concentrate on getting this day over with as soon as possible.

"So you and Stacey still hang out?" Jordan asks as he pops his head between me and Jeremy. My fingers grip the steering wheel in relief. He saw only a picture of me and Stacey. Wait! He snooped?

"That iPad is none of your business," I snap, and

then actually have to slam on the brakes in order to avoid colliding with the car in front of me.

"Watch it," Jeremy snarls as he recovers from bracing his arms on the dash.

"Sorry," I say as heat floods to my cheeks. We drive through the intersection at a snail's pace and then turn down the next street and park in front of the building. Jordan jumps out of the backseat and fills the meter with quarters before I even lock the car doors. "Thanks."

"No problem," he says with a smile that sets my chest on fire. His brown eyes move over my body, stopping on my chest briefly, before meeting my eyes. After being pregnant and then nursing Micah for a few months, my whole body changed. My hips have widened a bit, and my breasts went up a cup size. After the thorough glance-over Jordan just gave me, it makes me wonder if he has any idea what I've been through. What my body created, and how it's changed.

"Let's check this place out," I say as we walk through the lobby doors. We're greeted by a man in a suit who hands me a key to the condo and directs us to the elevator. I'm hoping Jordan and Jeremy like this place. It's probably the best-looking of the four I have to show them and, as an added bonus, it's fully furnished. We ride the elevator to the sixteenth floor and exit into a nicely decorated hallway with three doors, two on the sides and one directly ahead. The condo is on the right and, opening the door, I'm blown away by what I see. The pictures don't do the place justice.

We walk into a large living room with floor-to-ceiling windows overlooking downtown Phoenix. The floors are black marble, the furniture classy and comfortable, not to mention the black grand piano sitting beside the wall of windows. The kitchen is modern with gray cabinets and stainless steel appliances. Jordan and Jeremy explore the two bedrooms and bathrooms and meet me back in the living room when they've finished their tour.

"Tell me about this place," Jordan says as he sits on the cream leather couch, propping his feet on the marble coffee table.

"As you can see, it's two bedrooms, two baths, and comes furnished with everything you see here. There's a fitness center and pool on ground level, and rent includes house cleaning once a week. Also, the building has a restaurant you can order from twenty-four hours a day."

"And how much will this cost us?" Jeremy says from the kitchen. He doesn't look nearly as comfortable as Jordan does, and I can't help but wonder why. Does he not want to live with Jordan? I pull the lease information from my papers and walk it over to him.

"The lease price includes all these features and covers condo fees, parking fees, and concierge services. So, if you think about it, you're getting a really great deal. Besides, you can't beat the view." I step across the room and stand in front of the windows. "Imagine this at night with all the lights glowing from below. Imagine the sunsets you'll see from here. Remember how gorgeous the sunsets are, Jordan?"

A warm hand lands on the small of my back, and

I have to hold back my gasp. I glance up to see Jordan staring out over the horizon, looking lost in a memory. So many times we'd driven down to South Mountain at night and lay on the hood of his car, staring out at the sun as it dipped lower and lower in the sky. We held hands and remained silent as it disappeared over the mountains, setting the sky ablaze in magnificent pinks, purples, and oranges. I used to try to capture the colors with the cell phone camera, but the pictures never turned out right. Even now, I can't capture the brilliance.

"I really never paid attention to the sunsets." He sighs before his eyes find mine and then wander to my lips, stirring up lost feelings from so long ago. "I'm sorry I looked at your iPad. It was none of my business." His hand slips from my back, and the absence hurts, like I'm just noticing a piece of me that has always been missing—his mere touch completes the makeup of my soul.

"When can we move in?" Jordan asks from across the room.

"Don't you want to see the rest of the building?" I ask as we close up the condo.

"Nope. Just need to know what I need to do in order to live here."

"Jeremy, you good? Is this place okay?" He hasn't said much since stepping inside the condo and, since he'll be living here too, I want to make sure he isn't having any doubts.

"It's fine," he says with little enthusiasm.

Back at the office, we sort out all the paperwork, and I submit everything via email to the agency who listed the condo for rent. I asked for a quick response since Jordan's time frame is pretty tight.

"As soon as I hear from them I'll call you."

At three, I receive the approval for Jordan and Jeremy to move in as soon as today. My stomach twists into knots and my hands begin to sweat while I prepare to call them. I really don't know why I'm having such a hard time with this. *With Jordan.* It's not like I'll see him again—at least there really shouldn't be a reason to see him again.

I half expect to leave him a message after the fourth ring, but he picks up just as I take a breath. "Hello?"

"Jordan, it's...it's uh. You got the condo," I say, and then softly pound my fist into my forehead. *Quit acting like an idiot.*

"Yeah? That's great! When can we move in?" Is it wrong that every time he asks when *we* can move in, a part of me wishes it were him and me?

"Today if you want. The place is yours for four months."

"Thank you for your help, Reggie."

There's a pause and it's awkward, but I don't know how to end the call other than relaying how he can get the keys to the condo. About the time I'm ready to say goodbye, Jordan cuts in.

"I would really like to take you out to dinner. Will you go with me to Flancers?"

I haven't been to Flancers in years—it used to be our favorite place to go in high school when we wanted to feel like we were being fancy. It's really nothing more than a chain steakhouse, but the memories it conjures up are too much. I'm flooded with them, so much so that I brace myself on the edge of my desk in order to remain on my feet.

Could I go with him to Flancers? If I'm losing my footing based solely on memories, what would it be like when we walked in the building together like old times? Would we sit side by side like we used to, or would we sit across from each other like two strangers?

I shake my head, clearing away the confusion. No, I can't go out with him, not to Flancers or anywhere else. I've been living my life without him for almost nine years, and I'll continue to live this way.

"I really can't go out with you, Jordan." There. I've said it. Now maybe he'll drop it.

He sighs on the other end of the call. "Why not, Reggie-bug? Do you have a husband and a kid at home I don't know about?"

I silence a gasp as my hands begin to shake. I can't do this. Can't keep running into him.

"I have another call I need to take." It's a lie, but it allows me to hang up the phone quickly before he can argue or ask any other questions. Why, after nearly a decade, did he have to find me? Why can't I push these memories from my mind and slow my pounding heart?

Chapter 7

Jordan

Songwriting sounds so much better on a grand piano. That's what sold me on the condo. It wasn't the view or the fitness center or pool. It was the sleek black grand piano sitting dead center, the first thing you see upon entering. If the condo had nothing but the piano, I would've taken it—no question.

I play a few chords and runs on the ivory keys and listen as a melody forms in my head. The new album I've been working on will be a mix of ballads and rocks songs and most of them original Jordan Capshaw pieces. I haven't taken this much stock in an album since our first release. It's apparent with the drugs out of my system that I care more about what I put out to the world. Sure, my drug-induced music was good, but there wasn't any truth in those songs. They were merely words set to generic music someone else created.

But…this album. *This* album will be a part of my

soul I'm releasing to the world. My fans will finally know a small piece of the real me. The one who loved, who lost himself, and was then found. *Redeemed.*

The notes I play are laced with sorrow and heartache. Low on the register. But they build in depth and then flow into love and longing. The song reminds me of Reggie. It feels like the sadness I see when I look in her dark brown eyes, like the smile she tries to wear, though it doesn't reach her eyes. It feels like the slope of her shoulders and how they fell when she saw me at Eggceptional. I want to replace these feelings she tries to hide with hope and peace. And that's what this song is about. Turning something so sad and lost into something that looks forward to tomorrow.

By the time I've completed composing the melody and chorus, I'm exhausted. The lyrics flow freely from my brain and through my fingers as if they've been waiting to escape. It feels good to write music, to express what I seem to have trouble actually saying.

I haven't eaten all day. I find it's like fasting, and everything is clearer when I begin to compose. I dial up the guys and see if they want to meet at Eggceptional for a late dinner and to go over the songs. Of course, I'd be lying if I said I wasn't hoping to run into Reggie there. Jeremy and I jump in the car and drive across the I-10 and down Fifteenth to the familiar diner.

The guys are already waiting for us in the booth when we arrive. We slap hands in greeting and get right into hashing out the songs I've written, as well as the ones we've written collectively. I can't help but keep an eye out for Reggie. As the night trudges on, it seems she has the night off. My fists clench under the table and even as I try to hide my disappointment, it's written all over my face.

"Jeez, Jordan. Ease up or get laid," Drake groans from across the table. "You're just looking for trouble by coming here. That girl has moved on, and so should you."

"Shut the hell up," I say through my teeth.

"Let's just focus on the songs and then get out of here before Jordan bursts a blood vessel." Jeremy lays his hand on my shoulder, but I shrug it off and stalk to the restroom. Inside, I rest my hands on the sink and take several deep breaths in through my nose and out through my mouth. I run the tap and splash cold water on my face then count backward from twenty to zero. What is my problem?

Someone knocks on the door and steps inside—Jeremy. He's always coming to my rescue lately. Even though I need it, I'm also growing tired of it.

"Leave me alone, man." I pull a couple paper towels from the dispenser and wipe the water from my face. Jeremy stands against the far wall with his arms across his chest, studying me.

"If I wasn't living with you and practically riding your ass, I'd think you were either drinking or using again. What the hell is wrong with you?"

"That's just great, JD. I'm pretty sure that's exactly what the rest of the world will think any time I screw up. I don't need this shit, especially from the guys who are supposed to be my friends."

"No one's saying they think you're drunk or

high. We're just concerned. You're not acting like yourself."

The truth is I don't know what's going on with me. I'm on the verge of screwing up, can feel it deep in my gut. I haven't called a counselor like I promised Jemma, and guilt keeps pulling at me. The feelings resurfacing for Reggie that I thought I'd shoved away all those years ago confuse me. And to top it off, I'm pissed at my father—not that there's any shocking news in that regard.

I join Jeremy against the wall, but slip down to the floor and tug at my hair. Will I always feel like this? Will the craving and hunger to escape be a constant fight for the rest of my life? If it is, I'm pretty sure I'm going to lose in the end. I'm not as strong as I need to be against something so powerful.

"I know a guy who runs a Narcotics Anonymous group downtown. Maybe you should check it out." Since when did a simple statement from your best friend feel like such a punch in the gut?

"I don't need NA; what I need is for everyone to lay off me. If I want to come here to see Reggie, then I'll do it. If she's moved on, then I want to hear it from her, not from the guys."

Once again, Jeremy's hand rests on my shoulder, but this time I don't shrug it off. This time, he slides down next to me on the dirty bathroom floor and smacks the back of my head.

"Dude!"

"Did you really not know she worked at the rental agency?"

I shake my head. "I really didn't know."

Twenty minutes later, Jeremy and I regroup with the guys and work through the rest of the songs. We need thirteen for the album, which means four more before we can head out to L.A. to begin recording. And just in case the label doesn't like the thirteen we write, we need to have a couple backups.

It's after three in the morning when Jeremy and I return to the condo, but I can't sleep. Not seeing Reggie tonight really put me in a bitter mood, and I don't know why. It's odd, because I spent most of the day writing a song that *felt* like Reggie. Maybe it was too much of her. Maybe I need to focus on something other than her soft curves, long silky hair, and sad brown eyes. Or the way her rosy lips used to kiss the underside of my chin, feeling like a secret only she and I shared.

But then again, somehow I've been put in front of her twice in a short time. That has to mean something. Maybe it's a sign I should pursue her, show her I've changed and want to get to know her again. If she wants nothing more than to be friends, I think I could live with that, as long as I'm able to see her. Friends could work.

Yeah right. The minute some guy comes and sweeps her off her feet would be the minute he receives a right hook to the jaw and a busted nose. There's no way I'm letting some guy kiss the lips that had always felt made for me. No one else is going to put their hands where I've touched her. It's not going to happen.

The piano calls to me as the notes form in my head, creating the melody to a song about laying claim to the one you want. It's a song of possession and obsession. It's heavy, filled with the weight of fighting for what you want and not caring about those who get in your way. Jeremy has never lived with me when I had a piano to play whenever I want, and I've kept him up too late with my composing since moving here. I hope he's wearing the earplugs he bought a couple days ago, because if not, he's in for another long night.

Chapter 8

Reggie

"You seriously cannot go out wearing that," Stacey says, pointing her Perfectly Plum manicured nails at my apparently inappropriate outfit.

"What's wrong with it?" I don't think I look too bad. I'm wearing black leggings and a red and black flannel shirt that could almost pass as a dress in Scottsdale. "I even have a pair of boots I can throw on."

"You look like a lumberjack." Stacey's probably rolled her eyes at me at least a dozen times in the last hour. "We're going country dancing, not chopping down trees in the White Mountains. Come on," she says with a groan as she moves towards my closet. "I know you can do way better than this."

I don't know why we're going country dancing. It's not like we go out often, and besides, whiny, twangy music isn't exactly my thing. I'm more of an alternative rock kind of girl; I've always been that way. Well, ever since Jordan anyway.

Stacey returns from my closet and throws a couple things at me that I reluctantly accept. I strip down to my bra and panties and groan when I see the top she's picked out. I don't own any strapless bras, which means the girls will be hanging loose tonight.

I turn my back to her, remove my bra, and slide the top on, feeling a bit self-conscious. The white eyelet top hangs off my shoulders and cinches above my boobs. I pull on the pair of faded skinny jeans with holes on the thighs and knees and tug on a pair of camel-colored cowboy boots. When I glance in the mirror, I have to admit Stacey knows how to pick outfits. I guess her job in a clothing store is finally paying off.

Hair and makeup done, I give the babysitter one last run-down for the night, and then I give Micah a quick hug and kiss goodnight. I always feel so damn guilty when I leave him with a sitter, which is probably one reason I haven't dated in so long. That and the sheer fact I have a kid, and the look men give you once they know it is like admitting you have the plague. So, my options are fairly limited at best.

Our cab pulls up alongside the curb outside our complex, and I put on my pouty face and whimper a goodbye to my boy. Stacey smacks my shoulder—lovingly, of course—and we drive off into the night through the ever busy streets of Phoenix to the even busier Old Town Scottsdale.

Rowdy's is one of the only country bars in Old Town, and the cowboys come in droves on Friday and Saturday nights. The floor is scuffed from years of boot-stomping line dances and two-stepping slow dances and the quick-paced country swing. I really enjoy swing dancing. I love that most guys can pick me up and flip me over their arms and twirl me around with ease—sometimes there are some benefits to being only five feet four inches tall.

The bar is already crowded, and the night is still young. Apparently it's ladies' night, so our drinks are half price. Stacey and I push our way to the light oak bar and order a couple shots to start the night off and to loosen us up. There's an old saying I follow to the letter because it's always held true for me, and it goes like this:

> *Beer before liquor, never been sicker.*
> *Liquor before beer, you're in the clear.*

Not that I'm much of a beer drinker, but if I'm going to be mixing the two, I always start out with the hard stuff. We down two shots each of José Cuervo and make our way through the crowd to the large dance floor. Rowdy's really isn't much of a bar to be honest; it's more like two small bars flanking the dance floor so no matter where you are you're halfway to the booze. Smart planning on the owner's part, I think.

Near the center of the dance floor, Stacey and I kick up our heels with the other ladies dancing solo to John Michael Montgomery's "Sold." Our fingers are threaded through our belt loops, and we toe touch and jump, twist and clap. With the light buzz from the shots, we're having a great time. A few more dances down, and I'm ready for something a little fruity to hold me over for a little while. I motion for Stacey to follow me, and we shimmy through the crowd while a slow song brings out the couples.

I order a Malibu Cocktail, Stacey orders Sex on the Beach with her best bedroom eyes. She openly flirts with the bartender, who is admittedly pretty hot with his deep blue eyes and messy blond hair that looks like he's just gotten out of bed. In another time, I probably would've flirted as well, but I've got a kid to go home to, which leaves very little space for my own privacy.

Sufficiently satisfied with a growing buzz, I head back to the floor while Stacey continues her flirting. Halfway through "Save a Horse, Ride a Cowboy," a guy dances up next to me while everyone on the floor turns a one eighty. He's not bad looking, though his inky black hair is a little long for my taste and his brown eyes won't leave my breasts. When the song fades into a slow, steady two-step beat, he nods like he's asking if I want to dance with him. I figure there's no harm in it, so he spins me around and pulls me to his side as we move around the scuffed up oak floor.

When the song ends I thank him nicely for the dance and head back to the bar to find Stacey. Thankfully she's still there and, by the looks of it, two drinks ahead of me. She can drink me under the table any day, so I order myself another shot of José and down it quickly.

"He was cute," she says through lips that are trying not to laugh. She knows he's not my type, and she'll keep on teasing me if I don't give her a little bit back.

"Oh yeah, cute like a hairy Newfoundland who hasn't seen the sharp end of clippers in quite a while." We laugh and both shoot down another shot and head out onto the floor. We're moving in unison, sidestepping, kicking our legs out in front of us, and spinning a full circle while clapping to the beat, and I'm having so much fun. When the song ends and another slow one begins, someone taps my bare shoulder. Thinking it's Newfoundland guy, I turn with the intention of declining, but that guy is nowhere to be seen. Instead, standing in front of me with a smile that makes me melt is Jordan freaking Capshaw.

His hand moves up over my shoulder and reaches behind my neck where it sends a fire thrumming through my body, making all the blood rush to my cheeks. He doesn't ask, he just guides me around the room possessively. He's wearing a black cowboy hat, and the scruff on his face is somehow thicker, making him look like sin and heaven wrapped up in one gorgeous package. His black button-down shirt is open below his neck, revealing a fine smattering of hair he didn't have when we were younger.

He spins me around and I'm face-to-face with the one guy who can melt through every layer of the iron wall I've built over the years. One hand remains on my neck while the other rests on my hip where his thumb softly brushes against the bare skin just above the line of my jeans. Shivers alight all over my body each time his thumb moves, and I have to keep reminding myself to breathe.

Just breathe, Reggie.

In.

Out.

We move together through the songs, disregarding the tempo or style, unable to break the gaze between us. Our bodies move closer, comingling our breaths and synchronizing our heartbeats. I grip the shirt covering his chest when one of his legs moves between mine as the song slows. He pulls me closer, making the space between us nonexistent, and when his hips press against my stomach it's clear where his mind is at.

The song ends and I begin to pull away, but his hands quickly move over mine as he shakes his head and smiles a crooked smile.

"I'm not done with you yet," he says low and slow, pinning me in place. My entire body quakes as he dips his head and whispers in my ear. "You are the hottest thing in this place, and I want you all night."

Okay. Let's get one thing straight. When it comes to denying Jordan what he wants, my willpower is about as strong as a soaking wet paper towel trying to catch a bowling ball. Add that to the unquestionable number of drinks I've had tonight, and I'm pretty much guaranteed to do something I'm going to regret.

Chapter 9

Jordan

I told Jeremy I needed a break from being Jordan Capshaw and, given the whole world pretty much knows who I am, we go country dancing. Granted, there have been several country artists who have crossed over into the rock or alternative genres, but I've always been alt rock so I'm less recognizable in country bars. Add to that my growing beard and the black cowboy hat, no one really looks too closely at me.

We've frequented Rowdy's a few times over the years, though I've never done it sober, and was initially a bit nervous to do so. But after a couple dances with a couple nameless girls who did the whole, "You look a lot like Jordan Capshaw, did you know that?" I smiled brightly and donned my best southern accent and gave them a "Gee, thanks," before moving on.

Everything changed the second I saw Reggie dancing near the center of the crowd with Stacey, her hips swaying, boots stomping, and long hair swaying to the beat of the music. I was done for. Nothing would stop me from claiming her as mine tonight. Every guy here is going to know she belongs with me and there is nothing left to discuss.

After swinging her around the floor for countless songs, she tries to pull away, but I can't let her go. Her brown eyes search mine, and I'm so lost in them it's taking everything I've got to not kiss her. Then she goes and licks her pink lips, and I about lose it. My grip falters and she takes the opportunity to move away from me and walk toward the bar, making me groan in frustration as the natural sway of her hips taunts me. Apparently I enjoy torturing myself.

Jeremy finds me stalking my way to the bar and raises his brow. I shove him away and nod my head in the direction of Reggie. He rolls his eyes, claps me on the shoulder, and follows like a good wingman. Though, technically, I'm the wingman since he's drinking and looking for a hookup, and I'm not. Not that I wouldn't hookup with Reggie if the opportunity arose.

"Reggie!" Jeremy says a little too loudly. Both she and Stacey turn and smile, and hot damn Stacey's eyes wander over JD's chest as though she's on a slow journey across the hot Sahara desert. "Damn, Stacey, it's been a long time. How are you doing?"

Stacey's lips tighten into a slim line as her cheeks go from pink to rosy. "I've been good. Hey, Jordan."

Both girls sit on the stools at the bar holding

girly drinks that make my stomach roll. Reggie's drinking something fruity with Malibu Rum, and I begin to seriously rethink sobriety. Shit. My fists ball up in my pockets and I curse like a sailor in my head before turning away. It was a seriously bad error in judgment coming to Rowdy's, especially now that Reggie's here.

"I'll be back," I say, heading toward the door, needing a few minutes outside to keep myself from making a huge mistake. It would probably be a good idea to just head back to the condo and avoid the issues surrounding me right now. But when have I really ever listened to reason?

The crisp, late January air is like a slap in the face, and it feels good. After a few deep breaths, I decide I can do this. I can keep myself straight and watch out for my friends. I turn to head back inside and a warm hand falls on my shoulder. Reggie steps around my back and presses up against me, leaving little space between us. Her fingers walk up my chest, matching my rapidly increasing heartbeat, and stop under my chin. She sighs and runs her hand over my beard and leans in closer, landing her...*shit*. Her soft breasts press against my ribs, letting me know exactly how cold it is outside.

"Reggie-bug, what are you doing? You're not wearing a bra." My brain down south just woke up and has decided it's time for a jaunt down memory lane. Her glossy eyes follow her fingers as they move across my bearded jaw and down to the buttons on my shirt.

"I've wanted to touch your face since I saw you that first night at Eggceptional," she whispers, a smile playing on her pink lips. I can smell the alcohol on her breath, which would account for her sudden interest in me. "I wondered what it would feel like on my skin." She shivers against my chest and nuzzles closer. "I've wondered what it would feel like if you kissed me." She tilts her head back and gazes into my eyes.

It would be so easy. Kissing her. I could bring my hand to the back of her head and move it to where the kiss would zip through her toes. I could sweep my tongue into her mouth and see if she still tasted the same. It would be simple to lift her up and guide her legs so they wrapped around my waist, so I could show her exactly what her words and her touch is doing to me. But she's drunk, and kissing her would be like taking a drink, and I won't do that. As much as I want to kiss her and take her home to my bed, there is no way I'm doing that tonight.

"Let's go back inside," I say softly, brushing her silky hair behind her ear. "Stacey's probably wondering where you are."

Reggie glances up at me, and her brow crinkles in confusion. "I told her I was going to find you."

"And you found me. Let's get back inside. I've got to make sure JD isn't getting himself into trouble."

Her lips thrust into a pout as she rolls her eyes. "He's a grown man, Jordan. If he wants to screw some girl in the bathroom, let him."

"Shit," I say, pulling on her elbow to drag her back inside the busy bar.

"Let go, Jordan," she warns while attempting to

jerk out of my grip, but I hold firm. Once I find Stacey still at the bar flirting with the bartender, I tell her to watch Reggie while I go find Jeremy. He's not one to screw a random girl in the bathroom, which means he's had way more to drink than I realized. He's not in the men's room, and when I push open the door to the ladies' room, I hear bodies slapping together in one of the stalls. Glancing under the doors, I see two pairs of feet and then hear them finishing.

"Dixon, you asshat," I say as he stumbles out of the stall, zipping up his jeans and wearing an "I just got laid" smile. The blond girl stumbles out next, tugging down her skirt and pulling up her sequined, navy blue tube top. She smiles awkwardly and kisses Jeremy's cheek before leaving the restroom.

"Happy now?" I ask, slapping the back of his head. He smiles broadly and follows me out of the bathroom and back to the girls. He's going to be pissed at me tomorrow for letting this happen.

"You girls ready to call it a night?" I ask, placing my hand on the small of Reggie's back. She stiffens and then melts into my touch, and I'm suddenly jealous of Jeremy and his bathroom fling. I wouldn't do that to Reggie, but I want her so damn much.

Reggie turns to me, placing her legs on either side of mine and scoots close. Real close. Her fingers slip through my belt loops as she pulls herself up to meet my ear.

"Stacey and I took a cab here, and we're not ready to go. I want to dance some more, and I want more to drink. I want to forget for just a night." I know she didn't shout, but her breath wraps around my ear like an embrace; even with the music so loud, she's all I can hear. I glance at my watch. It's only a quarter past midnight, and even though I'd love to keep dancing with her, I think Jeremy and the girls have had enough.

"Everyone's had enough to drink tonight," I say, brushing my fingers across Reggie's cheek. Her eyes flutter as her tongue slides slowly across her lips. "And I'm driving you girls home, so let's go."

"Sober Jordan is no fun," Stacey says, pouting. "Jeremy here at least had a little fun of his own. Maybe you should take his lead and find yourself a little tail. You know I could just start shouting who you are and every single one of these girls here would drop their panties for you." She smirks and begins glancing around the room as though seriously contemplating shouting out to everyone in Rowdy's that I'm here.

"Real nice, Stacey. Showing your true colors. You've always been a class act." No use hiding my anger. "Keep on drinking, maybe you'll finally learn to close your legs. Oh wait, that's never been your thing, has it?" In high school, Stacey was known to be a little more than promiscuous. Rumor was if you wanted to have a good time with no attachments, she was your gal. Because she was Reggie's best friend, I never listened to the rumors when they flew my way and even did my best to stop them.

Drunk as she is, I can still tell I struck a chord with her. I'll admit, I feel bad. I don't know if she's changed since high school; truthfully I don't really care. But calling her a slut was a pretty shitty thing of me to do.

"Hey, I'm sorry," I say. "I shouldn't have said that. Can I just take you both home so you can call it a night?"

"Fine," Stacey says as she stands on wobbly legs. Jeremy's surprisingly quick on his feet despite being drunk and pulls her arm over his shoulder. Reggie leans on me as the four of us leave the bar and walk to my car. Reggie climbs in front while Stacey and Jeremy climb in back, and it feels like old times with my girl riding beside me. She stares out the window as the streets pass by. As soft snoring from the backseat fills the car, she finally turns to me.

"That was a pretty crappy thing for you to say to her," she says quietly as though not to wake our sleeping passengers. There is nothing more to do than nod in agreement; I've already apologized. What more is there to say?

"Were you following me again?" she asks after another few minutes.

I laugh because something obviously wants us together—call it fate or whatever, but Phoenix isn't a small place, and running into her like this is far too coincidental.

"Maybe I put a trace on your phone so I would know where you're going," I tease, but her head turns to me so fast I swear it's going to spin all the way around.

"Are you serious? I mean, I know you have a lot of money, but *did* you put a trace on my phone?"

"Right, because stalking is how I'm going to talk

you into going out with me."

She releases a breath as her shoulders sag. "You still want to take me on a date?"

"In case you didn't realize what you were doing to me on that dance floor or outside of Rowdy's, then I'll tell you flat out. Yes, Reggie-bug. I want to take you out on a date. I want to kiss you. I want you to know what my beard feels like on your lips, on your skin. I want to see if you still taste like I remember. And I want you to say that you'll let me take you out to dinner."

Her eyes widen and flutter closed, and her tongue glides over her bottom lip like she's remembering how it felt to kiss me all those years ago. Her mouth opens the smallest amount to let a sigh escape. And I can see I've won. My hands clench the steering wheel because if I don't hold onto the leather grips, I'll pull her into my lap and crush my lips into hers.

When we stop outside Reggie's apartment complex, I notice what a dive it is. Every kind of beat up car is parked in the lot, and the building looks older than dirt. I must have looked like a real prick to her when I asked her to show me condos.

Reggie turns around and leans over the seat to nudge Stacey, who opens her bloodshot eyes.

"Hey, we're home," she says before climbing out of the car. Jeremy is still passed out in the back, so I quickly step out and jog around to her side.

"I'll walk you up," I say, placing my hand on the small of her back. Her entire demeanor changes, and her back stiffens as she pulls away.

"No, Jordan. I don't want you coming up to my

apartment." She pulls Stacey's arm over her shoulder, who is leaning farther and farther to the left. Before she turns to go, she leans up on her toes and kisses my cheek, thanking me for the ride home. I move to follow her, but she scowls and shakes her head.

Chapter 10

Reggie

Micah assaults me way too early after the night out with Stacey. He's an early riser, like 6 a.m. early, and the swaying of my bed after he jumps onto it makes my stomach turn over. Why did I drink so much?

"Micah, honey, will you please get Mommy an ice cold cup of water?" He kisses my cheek and bounds out of my room as I trudge into the bathroom for three extra-strength Tylenol and then splash cool water on my face. I'm surprised my little boy didn't run from me when he saw the black mascara under my red-rimmed eyes. I'm never drinking like that again, no matter how much Stacey tries to convince me to.

Micah returns with the water, studies me with his head cocked to one side, and smiles wide as he wraps his arms around my waist in a huge hug. Times like this melt my heart and make me forget it's 6 a.m. and I have a hangover from hell. I live for this little human I created.

I spend the day doing errands with my little guy and end the afternoon at a park down the street from our apartment. I love watching Micah climb the rock wall and slide down the curvy slide, sporting an open-mouthed smile that reminds me so much of his father. The father who doesn't even know Micah exists—and I have no intentions of ever making him known.

Stacey is waiting for us when we return from the park and takes over my mommy duties while I change for my shift at Eggceptional. I truly dislike wearing the diner uniform of a short skirt and top, but Jim, the owner, is stuck on the idea that sex sells in a retro fifties diner. I kiss Micah goodnight, hug Stacey, and head to work.

Four hours into my shift, the door swings open, and my heart nearly leaps out of my chest, attaching itself to the man walking through. I kind of wish I'd drunk more than I did so I wouldn't remember how it felt to have his hands on me. Or how instinctively I walk toward him as though I'm a magnet and he's steel and we're drawn to each other. Or this smile. The damn smile that takes over my face when I see him or think about him.

"Reggie-bug," he whispers as he leans down, pressing a featherlight kiss on my cheek. "You look good."

That. Right. There. I'm a puddle of goo on the floor. My bones have been reduced to a gelatinous mess, my skin melts, and I want nothing more than to be the only thing he wants in this world.

Somehow, I manage to pull myself together and

show him to a table in my section. I hand him a menu, but he shakes his head and places it back in my hand.

"I know exactly what I want, Reggie-bug."

Yep. Goo.

"When is your break?" Jordan leans his elbow on the table. He's always been gorgeous, with brown hair that always seems to have summer highlights and brown eyes that are almost too big for his face. When I first saw photos of him sporting his scruffy five o'clock shadow on tour, I couldn't help but think it made his baby face less appealing. But time changes your outlook, and the neatly trimmed beard he has now is so damn sexy it makes my fingers itch every time I see him.

"In forty minutes," I say, remembering he asked me a question. "Why?"

"I want to ask you something." His lips turn up at the corners, and my stomach rolls over.

"You can ask me now," I say, pointing out the nearly empty restaurant. He shakes his head, gives me his food order, and winks as I turn and walk away. Forty minutes? I have to wait forty minutes to find out what he wants? Kill me now.

Somewhere in the span of those forty minutes, the restaurant fills up, and I don't have time to breathe let alone take my break. Jordan finished his meal a while ago, but continues to sit at his table while scratching some notes on a small pad of paper. Each time he glances up and our eyes meet, my stomach switches places with my heart. Finally, after almost ninety minutes, I'm able to take my break.

Jordan closes his notepad when I sit across from him at his table. He leans back in the chair and threads his fingers together behind his head, revealing well-toned biceps—yet another change for the better.

"You wanted to ask me something?" The air is thick between us, and I find it hard to be in the same space as he is, so I slouch in my chair and place my hands in my lap. My heart is thundering in my chest in anticipation of what I hope will be him asking me out. I already know I will say yes—I can't deny him or the feelings boiling near the surface. The only problem is Micah.

Micah, my son.

Damn.

I can't go out with Jordan. It's the worst idea ever. I swallow my anticipation and exchange it for the strength to refuse him. I already know this will be one of the hardest things I'll ever have to do. Not only because it's the right thing to do, but also because of how much I wish we could go back to how things were in high school. We were young, fearless, and in love. Time has changed things, and neither one of us has had it easy. I've had to make sacrifices to give Micah the life he deserves. I can't pretend none of these things exist or that it's possible Jordan's a ticking time bomb who might revert to a life of drugs and everything else I can't bear to think about.

Suddenly, it feels like a rope is pulling tight around my heart and squeezing the heck out of it. I can hardly breathe my chest hurts so much.

I make a move to stand, but Jordan quickly

reaches across the table and his fingers glide over my wrist to twine through mine. Heat surges up my arm and settles on my cheeks.

"It's only a date, Reggie-bug. Please let me take you out." His big brown eyes gaze into mine; he's practically begging me. I shake my head as the corners of my eyes burn with tears dying to escape.

"I can't," I whisper, pulling my hand from his. The loss of touch is like a rib pulled from my side— it hurts, and I gasp as the realization hits me: he's all there ever will be for me. No one else will ever be able to pull these feelings from me, no matter how hard they try. Jordan is like a parasite that not only makes me feel good, but damages me from the inside out.

Jordan stands when I do, and he follows me across the restaurant floor into the steamy kitchen.

"You can't be in here," I say with my back to him. The kitchen is cramped as it is with Rico cooking, but adding Jordan to the mix only makes the walls feel as though they're caving in around us. "I need to get out of here."

Rico raises a brow and points his greasy spatula at Jordan. "He bothering you, Reggie?"

I shake my head, give him a quick peck on the cheek, and tell him I need to leave.

"Okay, I'll have Miranda cover the rest of your shift."

"Thank you," I say, making my way through the kitchen toward the door leading to the alley. I open the door and hear Rico say, "Hurt her and you die." I choke on the tears trying their best to escape and slide down the brick wall, bringing my knees to my chest.

"Please don't cry, Reggie-bug," Jordan says as he sits down beside me, resting his hand on my shoulder.

"Stop calling me that." I want to scream at him. I want to tell him it hurts too much to hear him use the nickname he gave me so long ago.

"What can I do to make this right? I don't even know what I've done wrong." He runs his fingers through his hair, pulling on the soft strands, and emits a low groan of frustration. "What did I do to hurt you so badly?"

A sob bursts from my lips, and it's too late. The tears fall down my cheeks one after the other, landing on my knees. I watch as they slide down my skin, leaving trails of salty tears.

"Reggie, please. Tell me what's wrong." Jordan moves in front of me, lifts my chin with his fingers, and gazes into my eyes. "I need to fix this. Please let me." His other hand brushes the hair off my forehead and tucks it back over my shoulder before traveling back to my cheek. My eyes flutter closed as his palm flattens and his thumb softly, *slowly*, glides over my bottom lip, making me whimper. His touch is like my own personal drug, and I crave it like it's the only thing keeping me alive.

I close my eyes, savor the drag of his thumb across my lip until his lips replace his thumb in a whisper of a kiss. They are soft, warm, and a dam bursts inside of me, flooding me with every memory of the two of us I've ever locked away. The kiss is short—hesitant—and then he rests his forehead on mine.

"I never want to make you cry, Bug. Never. Will you please tell me what's wrong?"

"I can't, not right now." My hands move to his chest and he inhales sharply.

"When is your next night off? Will you tell me then?" he asks, his breath mingling with mine, swirling around us like a million fluttering butterfly wings.

"Thursday," I whisper, not understanding what's happening and refusing to open my eyes, knowing I'll break.

"I need to know you're okay," he says, pulling away. "I'll pick you up Thursday at seven." His thumb traces over my lips again, parting them.

Risking a glance in his eyes, I realize what he's just said. "No!" I nearly shout. "I mean, no. I'd rather meet you wherever we're going." A smile passes over Jordan's lips, and I seriously begin to doubt my sanity.

Chapter 11

Jordan

Bowling. Reggie picked bowling. I'm the man, it's my job to plan our date, but she picked freaking bowling. And she's driving herself. I'm beginning to think this really isn't a date after all.

I roll to a stop outside Bowlers, wipe my slick hands over my jeans, and give myself a mental pep talk. This is Reggie—there's no need to be nervous. I've played concerts for thousands of screaming fans and never felt like this.

Glancing across the busy street, I happen to catch Reggie stepping out of her car, and my jeans seriously shrink three sizes around my middle. She's dressed in black leather pants that show off her slender curves, and the shirt she's wearing—it's a silky gray top that wraps around her waist but is cut so low I can tell she's not wearing a bra. Is she trying to kill me? Her long brown hair is pulled up into a high ponytail that drapes over her shoulder. There's no way I'm going to be able to hide the rather inconvenient situation going on in my pants.

I close my eyes and concentrate on anything and everything that could possibly talk him down. Ice fishing. My great-aunt Betsy and her purple hair. In the middle of concentrating, a knock on my window breaks my train of thought and…shit. I can see straight down that low cut V of her shirt and the curve of her breasts—and there go my jeans tightening again.

This is going to be a long night.

Inside Bowlers, Reggie and I rent our shoes, pick our lane, and sit down at the table to order dinner. I haven't been bowling in years, and this place is a lot fancier than other place I've been. They have a gourmet menu, chandeliers, and by the gleam on the lanes it looks like they polish them after every round.

Every time Reggie leans over the table to reach for her glass of water or she ducks her head in laughter, I get a glimpse at her bare chest under that shirt and I truly believe tonight is going to be the death of me.

It's been twenty months.

Twenty. Months.

Before getting sober, I hadn't gone twenty days between girls. Honestly, I'm not even sure if he's performance ready after all this time. Somehow that doesn't even bother me. Sure, I've had a perma hard-on since Reggie stepped out of her car but, for once in my life, tonight isn't about sex. I'm on a date. I'm sober. And I'm having a great time. Twenty months ago, I would've walked out by now knowing I wasn't going to get laid. Now, even though I'd love to take her to my bed, I won't let it go that far with Reggie. It would be too hard to leave her when I go back on tour.

"Ready to lose to my awesome bowling skills?" Reggie asks as she stands and saunters over to the ball return to grab her ball. She leans over, showing me her perfect ass, and pulls a hot pink ball from the return and wiggles her hips.

"You're such a tease," I say, coming up behind her. She smells incredible, like cinnamon and roses, and the spice courses through me, warming me from the inside. I lean over and place my hand on the small of her back while I grab my ball. If she's going to tease me by shaking her ass, then I'm going to give it right back to her by touching her whenever and wherever I can.

"You're so going to lose." She struts to the lane, brings her arms up in front of her face, shimmies to the center, and glances back at me, wearing a killer smile. She takes three steps, bends over, and releases the ball, ending up with a strike. So, I'm going to lose. But I can at least be a man about it.

I hit the outer three pins my first roll and earn a spare on my second roll. And so our match continues, her getting strikes almost every turn, and me totally losing.

When we start our second game, Reggie walks up to me wearing that killer smile, showing off her dimples, and places her arms on my shoulders. She leans in and, for a second, I think she may kiss me. But she only whispers in my ear.

"I'll go ask for the bumpers this game," she says, and then pulls away, laughing at my obvious lack of bowling skills.

"Hey." My fingers close over her wrist, and her pulse speeds up as she gazes up at me. Reggie's chest is rising with heavy breaths; her eyes flit to my lips and then back up. My body remembers this. It remembers how she used to press up against me and run her fingers through my hair, driving me crazy. I'm doing all I can to keep myself from claiming her lips with mine right now, and it's killing me. I'm aching to touch her, to taste her, to see if she still makes those little sounds of pleasure when we're connected.

"Let's do this without bumpers," I say, clearing my throat. Her eyes fall as the moment passes. I can't tell if she's disappointed or relieved I didn't kiss her. She pulls her ball from the return and then passes in front of me.

"No bumpers, but you go first." She bumps her hip into mine, and her cheeks brighten.

"Come on, you remember. I always made you go first, and then at least twice." I wink at her, lean down, and give her a quick peck on the cheek and grab my ball. Her cheeks blush even pinker, and I step around her, square up, and release my ball, earning a strike. Game on!

"I've always been good at finding my mark," I tease, then smack her ass.

"It's easy when the target is so large," she shoots back.

"Do go on. Tell me how big I am." That gets a rise out of her, heating her neck and cheeks even more. "You know how I like to have my ego stroked."

"That's not all you liked stroked." Reggie lines up, shakes her ass in her black leather pants, and releases her ball. Halfway down the lane it ends up in the gutter.

"Now who needs the bumpers?"

In the end, she wins both games and it kills me that I lost, but I take it in stride and ask her if she wants to come to my place to watch a movie.

Chapter 12

Reggie

I should tell him I can't go back to his condo, quit while I'm ahead. I should go home to my little man, back to being a mom. But I can't—I don't want to.

I want to go with him and sit close while we watch a movie so that when I go home, my clothes smell like spice and musk and man—just like him. We've been flirting all night, shooting off lame sexual bowling innuendos that most would think are corny. But to me, they made my night. It's like these years we've been apart don't matter. We could pick up where we left off and be okay.

But then I think about Micah. I couldn't bring Jordan into my life without it affecting Micah in some way. And I haven't a clue if it would be good or bad for him.

Tonight. Tonight I'll enjoy our time together, and then tomorrow I'll return to my reality and remember the fun we've had. They'll be memories I treasure and will someday share with Micah. Someday when he's old enough to understand.

I follow Jordan in my car to his condo and work to keep my breathing steady, hoping I'll survive this night. We ride the elevator up in silence, each of us standing in a corner trying to ignore the growing tension between us. Our innocent flirting has somehow gotten us to a point that seems too big for either of us.

He unlocks the door. It swings open and the nighttime view of downtown Phoenix takes my breath away. The floor-to-ceiling windows overlook the streets, the flashing red, yellow, and green lights remind me of Christmas, when my parents and I would drive around looking at holiday lights. It's beautiful to the point of being almost intoxicating.

"How are you liking it here?" I ask, walking across the open room to the windows. If I lived here, I'd never leave this spot. "The view is incredible."

"Yeah," Jordan agrees from behind me. When I turn around, his eyes aren't gazing at the sight outside the windows, but down at me. My stomach swirls as his pupils dilate and he licks his lips. If he leaned down to kiss me, would I let him? Would I let this *thing* between us become something more? *Could* I let it become more?

His arms cage me in against the cool glass; his gaze turns my brain to mush. I'm back to being a puddle of goo at his feet, and it's a beautiful state to be in. My chest flutters and heats. My fingers long to dance across his skin, and my lips crave his.

Yes. I would let him kiss me. But I know it will

ruin me.

"Should we watch a movie?" I ask, nearly panting from the touch I want so badly but am terrified of. Jordan's forehead falls and rests on mine; his eyes close, spreading his inky lashes over gloriously flushed cheeks. We stand like this—stuck in a place neither one of us knows how to get out of—not knowing if we want to move away. Do we break through the barrier of lost years, or do we push these feelings of desire down and stomp on them like a fire that needs putting out?

"Reggie-bug," he whispers softly, his breath landing on my lips like a kiss from a ghost.

And...

I am...

...done.

I reach up, grasp the back of his neck with my fingers, and pull his lips to mine. The barrier has broken, the dam has fallen, and we're tongue-tied and lip-locked like our lives depend on this kiss. This one kiss that has shattered my heart, rebuilt it, and shattered it again. We move across the floor until the backs of my knees hit his couch, and I fall—him on top of me—with our mouths never separating. It's messy, hungry, and beautiful.

When his tongue finds mine, there's no longer room for thoughts. My brain has turned off and in its place is a glorious haze dominated by the feel of Jordan's scruffy beard on my face, on my lips. I thought kissing him with his beard would feel strange and awkward, but instead it's soft and soothing like a blanket on a cold winter's day. It's another layer of touch that sends tingles through my lips and chin, making me crave so much more.

He expertly grips my waist, turns over, and pulls me on top so I'm straddling his thighs, still never taking his lips from mine. I grip his shoulders, pressing my chest to his as he pulls my hips closer, leaving no space between us. He rocks against me, pulling a moan from my lips.

His tongue glides across my jaw, finding my ear as he caresses the outer shell. He pulls my lobe into his mouth and playfully nips, making me press against his hips even more. Jordan's fingers trace scorching lines down my sides until his palms rest on my upper thighs. His thumbs swipe across the front seam of my leather pants, and I nearly leap off his lap from the jolt it sends through me.

"Oh God," I whimper as my forehead falls to his shoulder. It's been so long since I've felt a man's touch *there*, it's a wonder I haven't completely lost it. Jordan's finger lifts my chin, and our lips collide once again. He holds me, possessing me like he's trying to convince me no other lips could be better than his. That a touch from any other will never hold a candle to this.

"This shirt is like a torture device, Reggie-bug," Jordan whispers against my neck. "Your breasts have been mocking me all night, and I think it's time they come out to play." He kisses a line down my neck, stopping at my shoulder to take a breath.

I gasp as he pulls the fabric of my low-cut shirt to the side and frees my bra-less breasts. He glances down, closes his eyes in appreciation, and then covers my left breast with his mouth. I jerk against him as his tongue flicks and lavishes me while his free hand kneads my other breast. I rock my hips against his and pull my lower lip between my teeth.

My body warms, welcoming the heaviness settling in my belly, delighting in Jordan's tender touches. My fingers run through his hair and pull him closer while he sucks and nips on my breasts.

"Don't stop," I pant, tightening my thighs, and pressing my center harder against him.

"I wasn't planning on it," he answers, dragging his lips back up to mine. His tongue delves inside my mouth while his palms help me grind against him. I moan into his kiss as the heat between us intensifies, and I'm so close to falling over the edge.

"Oh. My…" My breath is coming in short bursts until the front door flings open.

"This is just like in high school." Jeremy laughs, his voice dousing every spark trying desperately to come out of me. I'm scrambling to cover my breasts and hide the embarrassment covering my cheeks, while Jordan tries to shield me from view.

When I'm fully covered, Jordan presses a kiss to the tip of my nose and scoots me off his lap, but holds me close.

I. Want. To. Die.

Right here on this couch. Jeremy continues to laugh while he joins us, sitting on the other side of me. I pretend to find something in the lights of downtown Phoenix riveting.

"Relax, Reggie," Jeremy says as he pats my shoulder. "Nothing I haven't seen before."

"That may be true, but it's been years. Things…bodies change." I clench my teeth, trying to block out the memory of Jeremy walking in on me and Jordan making out in his bedroom when we were seventeen. At least this time I had on a bit more clothing.

"You look better now than you ever did in high school," Jordan says as he presses yet another kiss on me, this time on my temple. I may have just melted a little. If only he knew all the changes I've been through. How I grew a little human, and my breasts increased in size only to settle into what they are now. How my narrow hips spread just enough to birth a seven-pound baby, and how they never truly went back to what they were before I was pregnant.

Now that little human is home—sleeping—and I'm out on a date. Guilt is an evil thing. It burrows deep and festers like a parasite. Growing and feeding off the happiness you have until it's too big and suffocates your every agonizing thought.

I should be home, snuggling my little boy. Not here in the arms of Jordan Capshaw, the man who once held my heart. Who *still* may hold my heart. As Jordan uses the remote to turn on the TV, I stand abruptly, jostling the remote from his hand.

"You okay?" he asks as he leans down to scoop it off the floor.

"Yeah. I need to get home." I stumble away from the couch, grab my purse where I dropped it by the door, and turn around, colliding with Jordan's chest.

"It's only ten," he says, lifting my chin to meet his gaze.

"I know. I have a busy day tomorrow. Two jobs, and all."

"Are you sure? Don't let Jeremy scare you

away."

A laugh bubbles up from my throat—Jeremy scare me away? Hardly.

"No, I just need to get home."

"When can I see you again?" Jordan dips his head closer, moving his lips over mine. He's so close, each breath settles on my lips like a promise. The haze returns, and it takes all my strength to speak.

"Um, I'll call you?" My resolve is weakening, which is clearly due to the way the simple statement comes out sounding more like a question. I fumble, trying to find the handle, and when my fingers connect, Jordan's lips brush across mine. I succumb to the kiss, but only momentarily, until I can duck under him and pull the door open and slip into the hallway. I rush to the elevator, press the down button, and tap my fingers on my elbows as I wait for the doors to slide open.

Please don't let him come out here. I repeat it over and over until I can safely climb into the elevator and slink away from this place. I clamber into my car and receive a text from Jordan.

I miss you already. I want to see you again. Soon.

A sob bursts from my lips as I realize how easy it would be to fall back into a relationship with him. How kissing him feels like I've been waiting my entire life for him to return to me. But I'd be lying to myself if I thought anything could become of us. He has a band and a recording contract to think about; I have a kid at home who means the world to me. I'm not a carefree woman who can tour-hop with Jordan to try to make a relationship work. None of what we have is real. It's all a pretty fairy tale wrapped up in the lust-induced fantasy of Jordan Capshaw.

Chapter 13

Jordan

I couldn't put it off any longer. Today is my first appointment with a NA counselor. The first of many, I'm sure. I pull up to the white stucco building in the middle of the industrial part of town and think maybe more goes on here than just rehab counseling. If I were looking to score a big hit, this area would be the first place I'd go.

The windows are dark with sunscreens to block the hellish summer sun, and the white paint is chipping off the crumbling stucco. He better be worth the seventy-five an hour I'll be paying him.

Inside, I'm assaulted with avocado-green shag carpet and dark wood paneling covering the walls. Thankfully, the room doesn't smell like the seventies, but more like fresh cookies, which makes my stomach growl. Guess when you're high and have the munchies, walking into a building that smells like Grandma's kitchen goes a long way in convincing someone rehab is the right way to go.

"Jordan?" A man, about the age of my father, with salt and pepper hair greets me. He's about two inches taller than my six feet, and wearing a pair of khaki shorts, a green polo, and boat shoes. We're nowhere near a lake. "I'm Roger. It's good to meet you." He waves his arm toward a pair of chairs against the wall, and we both take a seat. Roger clasps his hands in his lap, pulls his ankle over his knee, and puffs out a breath.

"Tell me about yourself," he says as though he doesn't know who I am. I'm sure he googled me after I made the appointment, anyone would do it. *I* googled him. Roger Nelson, born November 16, 1960, in Riverside, California. Graduated with a bachelor's in psychology from Southern California University. He's married and has two children. His Google page looks like a fluffy, sparkly, pink page compared to my dark, black past.

Part of my rehab was learning how to separate my snarky rocker persona from the true Jordan Capshaw, and I still struggle with it when meeting people the first time. Today I'm going to do my best to be honest and get the most out of this session. So I begin with the facts.

"Twenty months ago I OD'd and wound up in the hospital. When I realized what I'd done and who I almost lost, I decided to give rehab a try. So far it's worked, and I've been sober and clean since then."

Roger sits back in his chair, nodding his head while I talk about my sobriety. I tell him about Jemma and how much I care for her. About how she's now married to Vic and will be having a baby soon. I thought it might hurt talking about her, but it honestly feels good to get it out. Roger sits back, listening, and appears actually interested in what I have to say. The counselors at the Warner clinic helped me a lot, and I feel like I'm in good hands here—despite the crappy décor.

"Why did you contact me? You seem like you're doing well."

"A week or so ago I was in a bad place. I had just called my parents and was yelled at by my father. It trigged an automatic response to drown myself in alcohol." A muscle in my jaw ticks at the memory, but I push through it.

"But you didn't drink. You dealt with the urge?"

"I called Jemma, and she talked me down from it."

"It seems like you have a set of good friends in her and Vic."

I nod in agreement. I'm not sure what I would've done without Jemma's rescue. I'm pretty sure I would've ended up drunk off my ass and out searching the streets for a dealer. That's what I felt like doing, but she reminded me of what I have to lose.

"How is your relationship with your parents?" Roger relaxes his legs, stretching them out, making him look like some sort of two-legged giraffe. I have to wonder if he played basketball when he was younger.

How do I explain my relationship with my parents to him when there isn't a relationship to speak of?

"There isn't much to say. I left home after high

school graduation and haven't seen my parents since. My father was angry I was pursuing my music career, and he forbid me to come home until I took a more honest approach to life."

"What made you call them a week ago?"

A laugh surges from my lips. "It was an accident, actually. Every once in a while my finger hovers over their number, and somehow I dialed without thinking. My mom answered, and I clammed up. I couldn't say anything to her. Then my father got on the line and yelled at me. At first he didn't know it was me, but when I spoke up, he laid into me. I hung up after the first insult."

"Tell me about your relationship with your father before you left home to pursue music."

I blow out a long breath and recount the bitter words spoken between us over the years. I recall all the times he told me I'd amount to nothing, how I was constantly disappointing him and my mother by the choices I made. I grew up hating my father, and it seems the feeling is mutual.

"Is there any part of you that would like to have a relationship with your parents?" Roger sits up in his chair and something inside me breaks. I don't know if it's the warm tone of his voice, or if he's just that good a counselor, but tears prick the corners of my eyes.

"Shit." I swipe away the tears with the backs of my hands.

"It's okay to *feel*, Jordan. With everything we've talked about, it's obvious you've dealt with a lot through your life. As men, we think we show strength by bottling up our emotions. Some make it through life this way and are no worse for wear. Others allow those bottled up emotions to fester and grate on us until we explode. Some go down the path of least resistance with drugs and alcohol; others take it out on the people around them."

Rogers pauses, places his hand on my shoulder, and squeezes. His lips form a thin smile.

"Just knowing somewhere inside you, these feelings of reconciliation and love are waiting to be released, gives me great confidence you're going to be okay. You're going to get through this and come out on the other side a better person for it."

"I didn't come here to cry like some chick," I say with a quick sniff.

"Crying doesn't make you a woman. There's great power in tears. They can be quite healing."

"Yeah. If you're a chick." We both laugh like old friends. We continue talking until my hour is up and when I stand to leave, Roger suggests I call my parents and try to begin repairing our relationship. I'm almost a hundred percent certain this will never happen regardless of how much I would like to see my mom. I have no desire to see my father and don't intend on taking anymore verbal battering from him. I can't take anymore.

On the drive back to the condo, I call JD and the guys and we make plans to go hiking in the morning. We're as close as you'd expect a group of guys who've been friends for years to be, but not hanging out with them regularly makes me miss their heckling.

I really put them through the wringer over the years, but somehow we've managed to come out of the dark better than we were. I love all these guys—they are the family I was forced to give up when we left all those years ago to record our first album. I'm grateful we made it, but don't think I can ever forgive my father for pushing me out the door and slamming it my face when I left.

I will never treat my own children like my father treated me. Not that I'll ever have any. I'm not really sure I'm father material.

Chapter 14

Reggie

Stacey and I have my car packed, Micah is buckled in, and we're loaded down with snacks for the six-hour drive to Anaheim. It's Disneyland or bust for the three of us. I promised my little boy I would take him on this trip if he could stop sucking his thumb, and, amazingly, the motivation worked. Score one for me!

We're pumped and ready for this little getaway—well, as pumped as two twenty-six-year-olds with a little man tagging along can be. Oh, who I am kidding? I'm just as excited as Micah, perhaps more. I haven't been to Disneyland since I was eleven, way before California Adventures was built.

The hotel we'll be staying at is only about five miles from the Disneyland entrance and was highly recommended by one of my co-workers. It's nice, very Californian with its airy, open lobby, Mexican tiled floors, and flowing fountains that only serve as a reminder I needed to pee about an hour ago. We check in, retrieve the key cards to our room, and walk down a path that leads past the heated pool, then to the stairs heading to our room. The smile plastered on Micah's face warms my chest and gives me one of those rare "I'm a good mom" feelings.

Our room has two double beds with fluffy comforters and soft down pillows. There's a small kitchenette and a decent bathroom with an oversized tub and shower combo.

"Dibs," I say, shimmying past Stacey, who shoots imaginary lasers at me from her brown eyes.

"Whatever. Just use the fan." We have no shame after being roomies for almost nine years. One of these days, my girl is going to be swept off her feet and strike out on her own, and it's going to be one of the saddest days of my life. She's been there every step of the way after graduation, all through me getting pregnant and having a kid. I only hope I can return the favor someday.

***

Whoever said Disneyland is the happiest place on earth was high on crack at the time. It's a parent's nightmare on caffeine and hyped up on sugar all wrapped up in a child-size terror-bot. We've been walking the park for almost six hours, my feet are killing me, I'm so sunburned I think my bones have turned pink, and I have a headache no amount of painkillers will cure.

And we get to do this all again tomorrow. Super.

By the time we reach the front of the line for

Space Mountain, Micah pulls on the hem of my shirt and tells me he has to pee. Why the park designers never thought to put a bathroom in the middle of the long-ass lines is beyond me. Like, why couldn't the line actually go *through* a bathroom? I know I can't be the first parent who has run into this problem.

Thankfully, the guys manning the ride give us a fast-pass that we can use right after Micah's done peeing.

Outside the restroom, while I wait for my boy to do his business, I can't help but notice the dads walking in and out of the bathrooms with their sons. A biting sting nags at the back of my throat knowing Micah could possibly never have this. He'll never know what it's like to have his father in his life. He'll never have a dad to talk about girls with or how to be a gentleman when dating. Even though I'll be there and try to talk about it with him, I've never experienced what a boy goes through, so it won't be the same coming from me.

And it hurts so badly to even think about it that when Micah skips out of the bathroom with an ear-to-ear grin on his face, I have to shove the guilt down deep in my gut. Instead, I kneel down and wrap my arms around him and hug him like it's the last time I can.

By the time we return to the hotel at nine, all three of us are too tired to use the pool and instead shower and fall into bed. My dreams are filled with the rides at Disneyland, but the typical Indiana Jones or Splash Mountain rides have all turned into carnivorous animals and snakes that feast on unsuspecting riders. It starts with the men, devouring them in bloody bites, then they start in on the children. Finally, I'm the last one sitting on the ride because I'm too terrified to move, and my heart has broken because I've lost Micah and was never able to find his father and show him what an amazing boy we created.

I wake up in a cold sweat, my head is throbbing terribly, and my throat is as dry as the desert back home in Phoenix. I check the clock on my phone—it's after four in the morning, and there's no way I can go back to sleep. I slip out of the bed I'm sharing with Micah and write a note to Stacey letting her know I'm going to the gym here in the hotel.

The gym is your typical hotel gym: a couple treadmills, stationary bikes, dumbbell weights, an elliptical, and something men often use with weights that resembles a torture device. I opt for the elliptical since it's a smooth run, and another day at Disneyland is all I need for pavement pounding. Fifteen minutes into my solitary run, the gym door swings open, and a guy walks in wearing a pair of black knit gym shorts and no shirt. He has dark brown, almost black hair, a smooth shaven face, and eyes that tell me all I need to know about him. He's pure lust wrapped up in a mouthwatering package. He lifts his eyebrows and quirks a smile in greeting and walks to the weight lifting torture device thing.

I'm not dead inside, and I'll admit when I change to the stationary bike, I watch him lie on the padded bench and lift weights. The muscles in his arms flex, and his stomach tightens as he presses the weights up, over his chest, and back down. He is gorgeous and, in another life, I may have approached him and flirted. But since Micah, I just sit back and enjoy the show.

We spend our second day at Disneyland standing in line after line, eating junk, and having a blast. If I never date again, it would be worth it to see the smile on my boy's face every time he sees Mickey Mouse or Buzz Lightyear. He's so happy, and that's what matters the most to me. I would pay a million dollars to see the grin he's had on his face since arriving in California.

Micah crashes in the backseat of the car about ten minutes after we leave Disneyland. Since I couldn't afford to take more than two days off work, we're driving back home after a hard day of Disney. After nearly an hour of driving and silence, Stacey turns to me, her lips drawn into a thin line.

"What are you going to do about Jordan?" she asks, keeping her focus on me. Her stare is making me uncomfortable, like an ant under a microscope. I realize I do need to do something about Jordan; I still have feelings for him after all these years, and I don't see them fading. But I have no idea how to deal with them, or if I should even act on them. He's a freaking rock star who's away from home for months at a time. I'm not sure I could handle a relationship where I don't see him on a regular basis. What would that do to Micah? What would Jordan think of my son?

Stacey clears her throat when I don't answer. "Well?"

"I wish I knew." We drive on with the radio

playing, and after a White Shadow song finishes I turn to Stacey. "What should I do?"

Chapter 15

Jordan

The guys and I have a small gig lined up tonight at The Roasted Bean, an indie coffee shop slash music house, and we're all anxious to get on stage. We ran through our set at my place and decided to include one of the new tracks I've written. There's no better way to test out a new song than on a small crowd. If they react well, it's a fairly good sign the song will do well overall. We load our equipment into the van, grab a bite to eat at a drive-thru, and then arrive at the coffee shop about an hour before show time.

I miss the rush of a concert. We've only been off tour for a couple weeks now, but the break can sometimes feel like an eternity. Except the days I see Reggie. Those days pass too quickly. How can I make them slow down? Better yet, how can I have more days with her?

"Yo, Jordan!" Drake calls, as he pulls his bass from the van. "You coming or what?"

I tip my head in acknowledgment and hop out of the vehicle. For a wealthy rock band, we should pay someone to transport our equipment for us, but when we're home, we feel somewhat nostalgic and use Jeremy's 1980s van. The paint has almost completely chipped off, the rear bumper is missing, and the doors squeal like a pig being chased by a wolf—but it's how we got started and how we like to remember where we came from.

Inside the coffee shop, the air is hot and thick with sweat and the musk of great coffee. It's not like the overpriced, burnt crap sold by chain coffee houses, but truly mouthwatering, addicting coffee. The crowd is decent, all huddled together like matches in a box and swaying to the music of some small-time, local band. They're young and remind me a little of us when we were in high school. Their lead singer, however, is female, and she wears her dark brown hair shaved on one side of her head while the other side sports long, skinny braids that hang down to her petite waist. Her voice is smoky and low, and as the song's tempo picks up, she growls into the microphone and I can almost see myself introducing her to our record label.

Maybe I will.

The guys and I haul our equipment backstage and chill out on the plush green leather sofas after doing a set walk-through. We sit and bullshit for a while until the mood takes a turn down a path I'd rather avoid.

"JD tells us you've seen Reggie a couple times," Grant says with a smirk. "You hittin' that again?"

The water I just chugged slips down my throat,

choking me. I cough, sit up straight, and fume while my temperature rises.

"Shut up, G," Jeremy says before I fully recover. He leans back against the dark blue wall with his arms folded across his chest. Irritation is laced across his face, pulling at the corners of his lips and turning them into a slight frown. "Get your head in the show and don't bring up Reggie again."

Grant's hands fly up in surrender while a shallow laugh bubbles from his throat. His cheeks blaze, but his eyes hold something bitter lurking near the surface. In the years I've known the guys, we've rarely had an argument we can't work through. Unless you consider the time they all kicked me out of the band. I didn't handle it very well. Then again, it helped spur my decision to go to rehab. Since we've been back together, though, all of us are a little quicker to snap and faster to bark.

Fully recovered, I turn to Jeremy, raise my brows in silent thanks, and then adjust my focus to Grant and the others. I want them to know that Reggie is off limits, not just because I've been out with her a couple times, but also because she's too good for any of the guys here. All of them—including myself.

"When it comes to Reggie, she's officially back on the *look but do not touch* list," I say, addressing Grant specifically. The way he ogled her in the diner makes me a little uneasy. Something in my gut tightens just thinking about Grant possibly having feelings for Reggie. I feel like a caveman staking my claim on her—like I'm beating the ground with my club and grunting my warning for everyone to stay away.

"Are you really bringing back that list?" Drake scrubs a hand across the scruff on his face and blows out a frustrated breath. "I thought we were done with that shit."

"We were until Grant here practically eye-undressed her in the diner."

"I didn't know it was her," Grant says apologetically. "I thought she was just some hot waitress."

"It doesn't matter. She's off-limits. End of discussion." I stand abruptly and excuse myself to use the restroom. We created the list when we first went on tour, and it was reserved for girlfriends or exes or really anyone we wanted. After Reggie and I broke up, I put her on the list because it's only natural to uphold the Bro Code by not dating someone's ex-girlfriend. Besides, I probably would've killed anyone who even thought about hooking up with Reggie.

The hall is lined with people just hoping to chat it up with the band coming off stage, and it's like trying to walk through a jungle filled with creeping vines. I push my way through—have more than one hand grope me—and find the bathroom. It's ripe; the acrid scent of stale piss stings my nose. I run the water in the sink until it's ice cold, then splash it over my face, letting the cool drops slide down my cheeks. I need to pull my shit together for the short set we have tonight—what the hell is wrong with me? I haven't been this possessive of a girl since...well, since Reggie. I can't afford to be distracted by her, no matter how sexy she is.

The bathroom door swings open, and the drummer from the band who just finished performing nods his head in greeting and then takes a piss in the urinal. I'm still standing here at the sink, my hands gripping the edge of the cultured marble countertop, letting my face air-dry. The guy stumbles over to me, digs through the front pocket of his jeans, and pulls out a small plastic bag containing a fine white powder—most likely cocaine.

My mouth begins to salivate, tempting me to pluck it from his fingers. My nose runs in anticipation of the high I know would feel amazing. My jaw clenches, hands tighten into fists, and I know I should get out of this place before I do something stupid.

"Jordan Capshaw! You jonesin' for a fix, my man?" the drummer asks with a smirk, and then proceeds to pull another bag from his pocket and hand it to me. "Have one on me, for old time's sake."

It's weightless in my palm, yet it feels like a ton of bricks. I stare at the bag—maybe for hours, I really don't know. I keep telling myself I don't need it, that I've been clean for twenty months now and I've beaten the addiction.

But.

The coke is practically singing to me, lulling me into a familiar pattern, urging me to take the release I've been depriving myself of for so long. I know exactly how it would make me feel, how it would zip through my body, lightening my step and putting my head in the clouds, relieving me of drama that just took place in the staging room.

But.

My hand fists around the bag, crushing the mesmerizing thoughts. Instead, I focus on all I've accomplished in the past twenty-one months and how I feel when I'm near Reggie. She doesn't need to see a wrecked Jordan—I'm better than that. I will be better than that for the rest of my life.

Jeremy pokes his head inside the bathroom; his jaw is tense. "We're going on in five," he says, his gaze sweeping over me. Like a child caught with their hand in the cookie jar, I'm riddled with guilt for just holding the bag of coke. I can't exactly throw it in the trash without him catching a glimpse, so instead I turn toward him, casually drop my hands to my side, and shove the bag into my back pocket. I'll get rid of it after the set.

On stage, we perform like we always do. The energy is high, the songs are solid, and the audience goes crazy. Singing onstage, no matter the size of the venue, is a high of its own. Who needs the artificial high sitting in the back pocket of my black jeans, taunting me like a monster lurking in the corner? I know it's there. I can feel its presence as though there's a spotlight pointed at my ass, alerting my band of the illegal substance hiding there.

I want to tear off these pants and burn them along with the coke, but I feel like I'd be betraying the drummer from the other band. I mean, he willingly gave me a cut, and it would be wrong of me to throw it away, wouldn't it? What would it hurt if I held onto it for a rainy day?

The guys and I head off stage, slapping

shoulders and teasing each other on our way to the staging room. The coffee shop has a couple guys to tear down the equipment, and no more than twenty minutes pass before the van is loaded up with the gear.

The coke is all I can think about. I don't even hear the conversation happening around me or notice when we pull into Eggceptional. I'm in a haze while we sit in our booth and order food.

"What the hell is that?" Jeremy says as his palm slaps down on the back of my hand, pinning it in place. The bag of coke slips out of my fingers onto the table in view of the band. I don't even remember taking it out of my pocket.

It's like we're transported instantly into a bubble and the only sound I can hear is the lack of breathing. No one is breathing. Not even me. Eyes. There are so many eyes boring into me, it feels like I'm shrinking. Or maybe they're all getting bigger.

"You've got to be freaking kidding me," Jeremy says as he fists the coke in his hand. "Twenty-one months. Have you been using all this time?" He shakes his head in disgust. "You're an asshole."

I know I have a voice. It's in here somewhere. In this body that wants so badly to betray my sobriety. I open my mouth to speak only to have a bubble of air pop out instead.

"I'm out of here," Jeremy says as he stands. "I really thought you'd cleaned up your act, man."

A fish out of water—that's what I am. Air is clogging up my lungs, locking in the words that should be forming. Instead, Drake, Grant, Carson, and Eddie join Jeremy in leaving me behind in the diner. Before Jeremy walks away though, he makes sure to throw the bag of coke on the table, once again giving it the ability to taunt me.

But.

I pull out my cell and dial.

"Hello?" Thankfully he answers. I need him right now.

"Roger? Shit, man. I'm in a tight spot, and I don't know what to do."

Chapter 16

Reggie

I've successfully *not* thought about Jordan probably six times in five days. Which means he's pretty much constantly on my mind. I've picked up my cell half a dozen times and started a text to him, only to delete it about five seconds later. I feel stupid. It's irresponsible of me to want to see him again, to crave his lips on mine. Just thinking about it sends shivers down my spine. So when a hulking figure looms outside my door at the rental agency, I bite the inside of my cheek to keep myself in check. I'd know his silhouette anywhere.

I shift papers around my desk to make it seem like I'm busy, check my reflection in the mirror I keep in the top drawer, and pop open the top button of my blouse for good measure. Was that really necessary? *Shit.* My cheeks heat with embarrassment at being so forward and, as I'm reaching to button my shirt, the door swings open.

Jordan's eyes roam over me, stopping at my

hands resting on the top button, and his lips curl into a cocky half smile. Damn. That smile alone makes me want to tear my shirt right off so he'll keep looking at me like I'm the only girl he sees. Like I'm a precious stone he wants to carry around in his pocket for safekeeping. The pocket of his skinny jeans that hug him perfectly.

"By all means," he waves his hand at my fumbling fingers hovering over the button, "take it off." He closes and locks the door behind him and steps around the desk. His palms rest on my shoulders, shooting wanton heat through my body, and if it weren't for us being here at my job, I would most definitely have done as he commanded. Instead, I button up, mentally kicking myself for unbuttoning it in the first place.

"It came undone while I was…while I had…" Lies don't fall easily from my lips; they never have.

"While you were doing what? Imagining my fingers running over your smooth skin, teasing you?" Jordan dips his head to mine, his lips a breath away from my ear. "You left in such a hurry the other night, we weren't able to finish." His whispered words flutter against my neck, sending goose bumps down my arms. Warm hands caress my shoulders once again, and then a finger burns a trail across my skin, following the line of my blouse to the top button. It pops open as though it has a mind of its own. *Traitor*.

Jordan's fingers slide down the center of my chest and then his thumb brushes over the front of my bra. I gasp, close my eyes, and revel in the way his hands feel like velvet on my skin.

104

"Come to lunch with me," he whispers. His lips brush against the shell of my ear and then trail down over my jaw.

"I can't," I say breathlessly. I don't trust myself with him right now. Every touch is too much, and it's corrupting my ability to think rationally. Jordan's lips hover over mine while his fingers trace the lace of my bra.

"Please come." He smiles, and I'd be a fool if I didn't catch the innuendo he's tossing at me. What I wouldn't do for a release like the one he's offering. Years. It's. Been. Years. It's not natural, and maybe even unhealthy. I should google to see what the effects of going years without sex does to a woman. "Reggie-bug," he whispers against my lips, and I melt. Yep. We collide. My arms wrap around behind his neck, pulling him hard against me. He parts my lips with his tongue, pulls me to my feet, grips firmly around my waist, and sits me down on the edge of the desk. Our arms are tangled, fighting for purchase, and our lips devour each breath. Heat explodes where Jordan's body presses against mine—hard meets soft and it's enough for me to know I want so much more despite all my hesitations.

Following my impulses, my hand trails down his shoulder, over his hard chest and down toward the hard lines of his stomach. My fingers graze over the bulge in his jeans, and a moan spills from Jordan's lips and falls into my mouth, where I swallow it and smile knowing just how much he wants me. He drives his hips into the palm of my hand, sending sparks of heat through my core.

"Regina, I have the Parkers here to see you." Reagan's voice rings out over the phone's intercom feature, breaking Jordan and I apart. I glance around the room, kicking myself for not keeping a clock on the wall.

"Shit," I say, scrambling off the desk and glancing down at my unbuttoned blouse. I forgot about my 9 a.m. appointment. Jordan laughs while I glare at him while buttoning back up. His cheeks are flushed, his lips swollen, and the bulge in his jeans is quite obvious—I can only imagine what I must look like.

"Lunch?" he asks as he runs his fingers through my hair.

I can't hold back the smile as I agree to meet him after my appointment with the Parkers is finished. Jordan leaves, kissing me quickly on my cheek, not satisfying me nearly enough. The tease. I give myself five more minutes before I greet the Parkers, a cute young couple expecting their first baby. We tour four nice condos in their price range before they settle on a three-bedroom, one-bath condo in Tempe near a great park.

When I finish with the Parkers, my stomach has officially tied itself into knots. I have to remind myself that we're only meeting for lunch. It's a public place, plenty of other people around. I feel like such a fickle idiot. One minute I'm rubbing Jordan's crotch and wishing that he'd just take me in my office, the next I'm nervous about eating lunch with him for fear of what might happen. I'm a grown-ass woman and should be able to do whatever I want. Or *who*ever I want. Why do I feel so guilty for wanting him?

I meet Jordan outside the office, and he surprises me by walking—instead of driving—to our lunch destination. Working downtown gives me an array of restaurants to choose from, and when Jordan opens the door to Bambino's Subs I raise my brows in approval. Bambino's has the most amazing pastrami on rye I've ever had. They pile on the meat, and the bread is made fresh daily. Just thinking about it makes my mouth water. The line to order reaches the door, but I don't mind waiting. The food is worth it.

Finally, with food in our hands, we sit at a small, round table and eat. Both of us ordered the pastrami sandwich, and Jordan moans when he takes his first bite, reminding me of being in my office with him this morning. My insides suddenly light on fire, and I can hardly concentrate on anything but Jordan's lips and how he licks them after every other bite. Or how his eyes roll into the back of his head as he takes another bite.

"What have you been doing lately?" I ask when I can't listen to him moan again.

His lips quirk into a smile as he leans back in his chair, studying me. "The guys and I just performed at The Roasted Bean last Friday and, honestly, it wasn't my finest performance." A muscle in his jaw ticks at the memory.

"You want to talk about it?"

"Roger says it's good if I do. Says it will help me stay clean."

"Is Roger your—"

"Sobriety coach. Counselor. Whatever. But yeah,

he's a good guy. I was at the coffee shop in the bathroom, and this drummer handed me a bag of coke. It was one of the worst nights of my life."

I swallow the lump in my throat, hoping the fear in my chest will leave. Drugs? I don't know what to say or do. I knit my fingers together under the table and let him continue.

"I didn't use, if that's what you're thinking. My band all thought I did, because I couldn't throw the coke away. I had it in my pocket all night, and it consumed my thoughts. After the set, while we were at Eggceptional, somehow I had taken it out of my pocket and was playing with the bag on the table. The guys seriously freaked out and left me in the diner."

Jordan's face is blank and pale, like he's reliving the night all over. I've never done drugs of any kind and have no idea what he must be going through now that he's clean. But I can imagine holding the very thing he's trying to stay away from must have been extremely difficult.

"What happened? Are the guys still pissed at you?"

Jordan shakes his head. "No. I called Roger in the middle of the night, and he met me at the diner. We talked for a couple hours, and then he brought me back to my condo. I woke Jeremy up, and Roger and I talked to him. Everything's fine with the guys now."

I blow out a breath and realize just how fragile Jordan is. Will he always be like this? Will he always struggle with the cravings to use or to drink? It didn't appear to bother him too much when he was at Rowdy's, and everyone but him was drinking. Guilt suddenly tugs at my chest.

"Jordan, I'm so sorry I was drinking that night at Rowdy's. I should have been more considerate when you showed up."

He smiles, reaches for my hand, and I give it to him willingly.

"The only thing I wanted that night was you," he says while squeezing my hand. *This man*. Goo.

Every.

Damn.

Time.

Chapter 17

Jordan

Each time Reggie and I go out, she insists on meeting me wherever we decide to go. I'm beginning to wonder if she has some secret at home she's hiding from me. I know she lives with Stacey, so that can't be it. Maybe since they're both chicks they always have bras lying all over the place, and she doesn't want me to see them. Or maybe she's no longer the neat freak she was back in high school and it embarrasses her. Whatever it is, it kind of pisses me off that I can't go pick her up like a proper gentleman.

What the hell?

Since when have I ever been a proper gentleman? Or spoken like one for that matter? I shake all thoughts of being proper out of my head, letting my long bangs swish over the bridge of my nose. I've been a little lax on hair care as of late, and since Reggie and I will be going out again today, a haircut and beard trim are in order.

Phoenix is a pretty large city, especially since the outlying areas have all grown together, leaving little space between zip codes. And therein lies the problem. There are hundreds of places I can go to have my hair cut, but most of them will probably sell me out to the paparazzi. That's the last thing I want, dozens of paparazzi trailing me around my city. After making some phone calls, Jeremy and I pull up to a fancy brick building in a ritzy part of Phoenix. Apparently they cater to the wealthy and keep their profiles low.

"Dude, this place is the shit." Jeremy whistles as we enter the building; some herbal mixture that would normally piss me off immediately assaults our senses. But instead, the scent is soothing and almost makes me sleepy. The walls look like vanilla ice cream; the floors sparkle like milky diamonds. What kind of place have we come to?

"Welcome to Rohipsy, Mr. Capshaw. My name is Brandy." What is with this place and all the cream? The woman greeting us has hair the color of the walls, a tan she must have bought, and a smile straight out of a magazine. "We're so glad you've come to us today. Won't you both follow me?"

Brandy struts her Manolo Blahniks across the floor and shows us to a steam room where she explains the process of Rohipsy. Two and a half hours later, I'm thoroughly steamed, washed, cut, and trimmed and smell something like the lavender and eucalyptus they feed through the air vents.

"Well. That was something," I say as Jeremy and I climb into the car. He only nods, and when I glance back at him, he's looking a little green. "You okay?"

"The chick who cut my hair," he begins, becoming paler by the second. "I, uh…we. She was the girl from Rowdy's, dude."

"The girl from…" *Oh.* "Did you remember her? I mean, you know, you were pretty wasted."

Jeremy groans, clamps his eyes shut, and lets his head fall back against the headrest. I take that as a no.

"She asked me out." His throat bobs, and I laugh. I can't help it. He looks sick, like thinking about going out with this chick might kill him. His fist connects with my shoulder as I pull onto the road.

"Is that a bad thing? She looked pretty hot, and there wouldn't be any awkwardness between you guys since you already hooked up."

"I don't hook up, dude. That's always been your thing."

It was what I always did. I'd been doing it for years since going on tour and never giving it half a thought. But when I met Jemma, everything changed. Sobriety really makes you look at life differently. I've hated that part of myself for a long time now and wish I could take all of it back. At least I was smart enough to wear a condom every damn time. Even drunk and high as a kite, I made sure of that. I don't know what I would do with tiny Jordan Capshaws running around. I shake my head at the thought and shudder.

"Sorry," Jeremy says when I don't respond.

"Hey, don't worry about it. I deserved that."

He shakes his head. "No. You've turned yourself around, and you should be proud of yourself."

Am I proud of myself? Does staying clean for almost two years mean I've hit some milestone that says I can pat myself on the back and forget past wrongs? It wasn't even a week ago I held a bag of cocaine in my hand and couldn't throw it away. No. I'm not proud of myself. I can't stomach myself sometimes.

"You going to go out with her?" A change of subject is needed. Wallowing in my own guilt isn't a good way to get ready for my date with Reggie.

Jeremy sighs, long and breathy, drags his hands across his freshly shaven face, and puffs out his cheeks. "Yeah. I guess."

"When? Wanna double with me and Reggie tonight?" Wait. I don't want them to double with us. I want Reggie all to myself.

Before I can retract my offer, Jeremy says, "Sure. I'll shoot her a text and find out if she's cool with it."

Turns out the chick, Emily, was very much okay with doubling with me and Reggie. The four of us meet up at El Casa Viejo, and of course Jeremy and I arrive fifteen minutes before Reggie shows up wearing a strapless red dress that hugs her body like it was painted on. Her long hair is curled in waves that cascade over her back, and I'm pretty sure I'm going to have to give her the shirt off my back because every guy in here won't be able to keep their eyes off her.

Reggie quickly swipes her tongue across scarlet lips, brushes an imaginary stray hair behind her ear, and studies the cracks in the patio. I lean in, inhale her flowery scent, and whisper in her ear just how amazing she looks. Her cheeks flush as my fingers trail down her arm before I twine my fingers with hers.

"Shit," Jeremy says as he thrusts his hands in his pockets and jerks his chin towards a blond-haired girl walking this way. "She looks good." Her long legs look even longer in a black skirt that shimmies as she walks.

"Hey," Jeremy says as Emily moves to stand near him, but not close enough you'd think they'd been as friendly as they were a couple weeks ago.

"Hi." Emily tugs at the hem of her dress as we walk through the restaurant to our table. She appears just as nervous as I know Jeremy is. Reggie loops her arm through mine and pulls me beside her in the high leather booth. Emily and Jeremy join us, keeping a good two feet between them. Awkward.

"You boys sure clean up well," Reggie says after she's thoroughly inspected my haircut and beard trim. I don't miss the way her fingers trail over the nape of my neck and glide into the bottom of my hair. The touch zings through me, settling between my legs. Yes. It's been twenty-one months since I last had sex. Yes. I want to have sex with Reggie. I would be lying if the thought hasn't crossed my mind every day since seeing her at the diner. But with our history, I'm not sure we should cross that line again with me leaving so soon to go back on tour.

Reggie's fingers remain at the back of my neck, twirling in the short hair, and I physically have to pinch my thigh until I want to scream in order to keep from needing to adjust myself under the table.

Our waiter comes for our drink order and even though he obviously knows who I am, keeps his cool. Sometimes I wonder if Jeremy feels a little left out in the grand scheme of things. As band manager, he's as much a part of the band as I am, but his part is all behind the scenes. He'll never receive the recognition the guys or I do.

"How do you two know each other?" Emily asks me and Reggie. When our drinks arrive—water for me and Reggie, sodas for Emily and Jeremy— Emily inches a bit closer to Jeremy.

"We all went to high school together," Jeremy says after he takes a drink. "They were high school sweethearts."

Emily beams at us, her cheeks lighting up. "Really? That's amazing. You guys have been together all this time?"

I nearly choke on my water as Reggie's fingernails scratch my neck. I turn to her, notice the red in her cheeks, and shrug.

"We broke up after graduation," I clarify. "I went on tour with the guys, and Reggie's been working." The conversation throughout dinner is like this. Back and forth exchanges, all while every few minutes Emily and Jeremy inch closer to each other. By the time we pay the check, they're sitting as close as Reggie and I are. Which is to say we're hip to hip.

As we leave the restaurant, we decide to all file into my car and head to Rowdy's for dancing. The club is packed, and I'm swarmed with a group of girls not twenty feet inside the building. Jeremy runs interference, directs our small group toward the center of the dance floor, and whistles. When I say whistles, I mean he blows out an earsplitting, chalkboard screeching whistle everyone around us can hear even above the music.

"Listen up!" he shouts, pulling everyone's attention to where the four of us are standing. "I have *the* Jordan freaking Capshaw standing here with his girl, Reggie. Give us some dancing room or get the hell out of here. And unless you want me to call our security squad, leave us alone."

The club goes dead silent, like chirping crickets silent, before the music begins pumping through the speakers once again and the crowd returns to two-stepping around the weathered oak floor.

"Was that really necessary?" Reggie asks as I pull her around and grip the tight red fabric at her hip, inching the short hemline up an inch or so.

"Yep."

Chapter 18

Reggie

Jordan's fingers don't leave my hip as we glide across the floor. He's possessive, hot, and the way his dark blue henley tugs across his chest makes my knees weak. "To Make You Feel My Love" by Garth Brooks plays over the speakers, and he pulls me even closer, dragging my legs around his thigh, inching my already short dress higher. I tug on the hem, but his eyes find mine, and his lips turn up in a seductive grin. He shakes his head and reaches for my hand, guiding it to his chest, over his heart. The rhythm is heavy and fast, and it echoes my own.

I know I'm in trouble. I knew that the moment I saw Jordan at the diner. But I don't know if I'm the only one. Sometimes he looks at me like I'm his whole world, like he sees only me and nothing else matters. But then there are times I see something else. Something foreign and almost terrifying. He'll gaze off into the distance, lips pursed, nostrils flaring, and his soft brown eyes looking at anything

117

but me.

Even though he's holding me in his arms on this dance floor, the look he has on his face right now scares me. It's fierce, and possessive, and hungry. His grip on my hip and my hand pulses heat through me, making me feel lightheaded. We turn and spin on the dance floor, and when our eyes connect, neither one of us can look away. His fingers dig into my hip, while his other hand glides down my arm and falls to the back of my neck.

It's as though the room clears, and there's no one left in Rowdy's except for us. The music is playing; Garth Brooks is lulling us closer—even though I don't know how it's even possible. And we dance like we're stripping our souls for one another. Baring our inner demons, laying claim with our touch, and whispering promises with our ragged breath.

Jordan dips his head lower, his forehead rests on mine, and we both close our eyes because it's all too much. He brushes his lips across the tip of my nose and slides his cheek to meet mine.

"I don't know what I'm doing here, Reggie-bug." Even though he whispers the words, I hear them loud and clear. My stomach clenches and drops, fearing he's somehow telling me he doesn't want this, doesn't want me. But his arms pull me into his chest, and he turns his head to press his lips against my ear. "Tell me to take you back to my place. Tell me you want me as much as I want you."

I do want him—want *this*. I sigh into his cheek, and wet my lips in hungry anticipation. My fingers graze his chin, pulling his face to mine and his eyes reflect what I'm feeling—longing. I swallow slowly, dipping my eyes to his mouth, and pull him closer. My answer comes in the form of a warm breath on his eager lips, a gentle sigh that brings us closer, and a soft caress of my tingling lips on his.

Jordan's eyes close in relief, his hand finds mine, and he guides me through the crowd until we find a very cozy Emily and Jeremy dancing.

"Reggie and I are going to cut out of here," Jordan says to Jeremy, pulling his car keys from his pocket. Jeremy glances between me and Jordan, then turns to Emily as a grin spreads across his knowing face.

"We'll grab a cab back to the restaurant," he says with a laugh.

"No, take my car." I say, handing him my car keys so he'll have something to drive home when he and Emily are finished with their date. Whose great idea was it to take separate cars anyway? Right...mine. Oh shit, things are getting real, really fast. Jordan ducks down, brushes his lips across my cheek, and pulls me toward the front door. Am I really going to do this? I mean, I'm prepared...physically. All smooth, plucked, and fresh. So why does my stomach feel like it's preparing to run an epic marathon?

Jordan pulls me around in front of him and backs me against his car. His eyes search mine for, I don't know—permission? He drags a finger across my bottom lip, wets his own, and leans in close. The tips of our noses brush together, and when the soft flesh of his lips meets mine, a sigh is unavoidable. The kiss is slow and light, as though he's making

119

sure this is what we both want. It is, isn't it? Do I really want this? Do I want Jordan between my legs, on top of me, possessing me?

The kiss grows more desperate, our bodies press together against his car, and yes, I do want this.

"Take me home, Jordan," I whisper as our lips break apart. He stands upright and backs up a step, looking at me like I've just asked him to fly me to the moon. His mouth bobs somewhere between open and closed, and I realize he must think I mean back to *my* home.

Smiling, I trail my fingers down his chest, stopping at the top of his jeans. I drag my finger through a belt loop and pull his hips against me.

"I meant take me back to your place. I'd rather not give the good people of Scottsdale a show."

Jordan drives erratically through the city streets until we reach the freeway. While he's driving, I send a quick text to Stacey to let her know I'll be home sometime in the morning and tell her how amazing she is for taking care of Micah. I feel a little like I'm breaking curfew and I'm going to get caught. Maybe this isn't such a good idea.

My stomach rolls, making me feel a little queasy now that reality is settling in. Jordan twines his fingers with mine as we park outside his condo.

"You okay?" he asks as he pulls my hand to his lips and kisses gently.

I nod, swallow the lump in my throat, and decide to put on my big girl panties. It's only sex. With Jordan. My ex. It's not like we haven't done this before.

In the elevator, Jordan brushes the hair off my

neck, sending shivers down my spine. His hand is so warm on the back of my neck and, as possessive as the gesture may be, it makes my insides tingle.

"We can just relax and watch a movie if this is too much for you, Reggie-bug." He squeezes the back of my neck gently, and then trails the tips of his fingers down my back before they stop at my waist. He tugs me gently into his side and kisses the soft spot below my neck. The elevator doors glide open, and I take a deep breath. I can do this.

Inside the condo, I quickly excuse myself to use the restroom. While inside, I marvel at the expensive tile and sparkling quartz counters. Even the shower has bits of shiny glass or crystal of some kind. I rest both palms on the sink counter, take several deep breaths, and then do a quick odor check. I must have put on about ten layers of deodorant before getting dressed tonight. Everything smells good and fresh, despite how clammy my body feels.

Do I confess to him just how long it's been for me? That even though it's been years for us as a couple, I still remember how he felt? Though, despite being a really great kisser in high school, his kisses now blow those out of the water. What if sex is even better now than it was then?

Maybe I swallowed a hummingbird. Maybe what I feel in my chest is the poor bird trying desperately to be free of the cage my ribs have become. Maybe I'm going to be sick.

And then the sweetest notes on a piano echo through the walls of the bathroom. The melody is beautiful and suddenly makes me emotional. Like

121

the music I know Jordan is playing is a song he wrote just for me. I can feel the notes wrapping around me like a hug, and it's amazing, almost intoxicating.

I join him at the piano, watch as his long fingers dance over the shiny white keys, and the music flows freely. He's humming a tune I don't recognize, yet it feels so familiar. When the song finishes, Jordan turns to me, runs his fingers through my hair, and trails them down my jaw to my bottom lip. A sigh escapes me as his other hand reaches for my cheek. His gaze lingers on my eyes then falls to my lips, before he lowers his head and grazes his lips over mine.

Somehow, the raging hunger has died, but it's been replaced by a tender desire that slowly climbs higher and higher as Jordan pulls me onto his lap, my legs straddling his. His hands rest firmly on my hips as his lips continue to set the pace. There's no rush, no tongue, just the soft, gentle pressing of his warm lips against my skin.

This kiss has got to be my new favorite.

But then, as if his patience is waning, his tongue parts my lips and seeks entrance into my mouth. His tongue twists against mine, pulling at me until he coaxes my tongue into his mouth, and I'm lost. I've fallen into the abyss that is Jordan and no longer feel the heaviness of my life. There's only him and me and this moment where we're speaking through the rocking of hips and the searching of tongues. Hungry hands slide up my back, over my shoulders, and down the front of my dress, grazing my breasts as he passes down to the tops of my thighs.

A moan passes through my mouth into his, and the kiss deepens. Jordan's hands slide to my thighs then move below my butt, pulling yet another moan from me. His grip tightens as he stands abruptly, wraps my legs around his waist, and sends the piano bench sliding across the floor. I grip the back of his neck as his hold on me stays firmly on my butt, and we continue to kiss all the way to his bedroom.

Chapter 19

Jordan

If I don't pace myself, I'm going to blow my load in my jeans. Reggie's firm ass in my hands feels crazy good. Her red dress has slid so far up her legs that she might as well not be wearing it. If I have anything to say about it, she'll be out of it in about ten seconds. Kissing her like that on the piano bench, like she's all mine and there's nothing anyone can do about it, was almost too much—like I'm diving too deep. It felt so damn good, and the warmth from between her thighs pressing down on me was…I've got to stop thinking about it.

I have her in my arms. My lips are still on hers, my tongue in her mouth, and the way she sucks on it like it's a lollypop is making my pants way too tight. I love the soft whimpers that fall from her lips when I press my hips into her center, showing her exactly how much I want her. How kissing her like this is driving me crazy.

She unwraps her legs from my waist, slides

down to the floor, and traces her fingers along my stomach, making my muscles tighten as she stops at the top of my jeans and pulls my bottom lip into her mouth. Her tongue swipes over my lips before she pulls away, turning her back to me. I run my hands down her sides, stopping at her hips, and pull her ass against me. She gasps, her cheeks flush, and she bites the inside of her cheek to stop from smiling.

We were good together in high school—really good. But as good as we were, I've changed, and I'm sure Reggie has too. What was a tender, slow act with Reggie in high school, was erased by the drugs and turned into something frantic, almost manic, with every girl after her. It was never about pleasing the girl I was with, but only getting myself off no matter how fast or impersonal. I lost count after our second year of touring, deciding the numbers didn't matter, especially since the girls remained nameless.

Tonight, being with Reggie, it's not like it was with the others. I want to take my time. I want to make her feel as good as she's making me feel.

Reggie brings her hand to my jeans and slowly glides her fingers over the front zipper, and I actually have to pull away from her. *This girl.*

"Hey, Bug, let me touch you," I say as she gazes up at me, her dark eyes wide with uncertainty. "It's been a long while for me, and you're feeling too good. If you keep touching me like that, this is going to be over before we even begin."

A pale pink blush settles on her cheeks as she smiles on one side of her mouth. She nods and slowly walks across the floor to sit on the edge of the bed. She leans down, removes her nude heels and holds the strappy shoes by a finger. They sway against her hand before she glances up to me and tosses them across the room. I flip the light switches, turning off the overhead light, changing everything to the pale glow of the table lamps. I want to see every inch of this woman.

I stand across the room, staring at her tan, lean legs, and then my eyes travel up her red dress to her perfect breasts. Her chest is rising and falling in deep breaths. Am I making her nervous? Her fingers tug at the hem of the short dress, and suddenly I'm thrust back into a memory when I was sixteen, sitting with Reggie in my bedroom at my parents' home. We were both nervous because we decided to have sex for the first time. We'd perfected kissing; I'd felt her up and even touched her intimately. But we were going all the way.

Reggie is wearing the same look right now as she did all those years ago. Surprisingly, I'm almost as nervous as I was then too. I mean, I know what I'm doing now, but what if she's had better since me? Or what if I'm too rough?

Shit. I run my hands through my hair, tugging at the shortened tresses, and join Reggie on the bed. We both sigh, not knowing exactly how to move forward. I don't want to ruin this—ruin what's growing between us.

Reggie sighs once more and then says, "It's been a *really* long time for me too." There is a lot of emphasis on *really*, making me wonder just how long it's been. Her tongue slowly runs over her plump lips and then she gazes at me before taking a deep breath. Her lashes flicker and my resolve crumbles. My hands move to her cheeks, and I pull her face to mine, my mouth claiming hers. Gone is the softness. Gone is the slow, tender kiss. Instead, what's between us is frenzied, hungry, and full of soft moans of pleasure.

I move over her, lie her back on the bed, and place my knee at the juncture of her thighs. Her dress rides up, showing off her lacy red panties, and the heat between her legs urges me on. Her fingers pull my shirt up to my shoulders, and I sit up, tossing it across the room to join her shoes. She quickly removes my belt, unbuttons my jeans, and slides her hand beneath my boxers. I hiss at the contact, jerk away, and then return my lips to hers.

"I need to be inside you right now," I say against her gaping mouth. "I'm sorry, but this is going to be quick."

She nods and scoots up to the head of the bed, gazing at me with hooded eyes. She's beautiful with her hair askew, hanging over one shoulder. I slide my jeans and boxers off, and Reggie's eyes widen for a brief moment. I smirk a little, knowing my chest and shoulders aren't the only things that gained some size after we broke up. I pull a condom from the nightstand—at least I was prepared—slide it on, and climb over her.

Our lips meet, her hands wrap around my neck and suddenly…I'm home. There is nothing hurried about this. It's slow and tight and, good God, it's *so good*. Her legs wrap around my hips. She tilts up and gasps, clawing at my back. Reggie bucks forward as I hit her just right; her teeth connect with

127

my shoulder, and she clenches around me, squeezing until I collapse on top of her.

I don't want to move, don't want to slide out of her ever again. She feels too damn good. But I do. I'm breathing heavily; my forehead is dotted with sweat. I kiss her again—her lips, the tip of her nose, her forehead. I place a kiss all over her flushed skin until she's begging me to slide inside her again. And I do.

Chapter 20

Reggie

The early alarm on my phone makes me groan in protest. *Last night.* My cheeks heat remembering Jordan's touch, how he felt inside me. How is it possible for him to be even bigger than he was in high school? Not that I'm complaining—I'm sore in the best way.

Jordan rolls over, and his arm drapes over my waist, pulling me back against his chest. His lips drag across my neck as he presses his hard length between my thighs.

"Once more before you go?" he asks, pulling my leg over his. His hand moves up my waist, cups my breast, and he glides inside me. Heat blossoms on my cheeks, my stomach tightens, and I'm rocking against him. And then I'm there, so quickly it's like he flips a switch, and I'm squeezing him and gasping. He pulls out and then mutters a curse before rolling over to sit on the edge of the bed.

"I, uh…damn, Reggie-bug. I'm sorry. I wasn't

thinking." He grips the sheets while clenching his jaw.

I sit up, pull the sheets over myself, and swallow the lump forming in my throat. "What's wrong? Did I do something?"

He moves quickly beside me, pulls me into his chest, and sighs. "No, Bug, it wasn't you. I just got caught up in the moment and didn't use a freaking condom. I'm clean, babe. I got tested while I was in rehab."

He didn't use a condom? My heart takes off in my chest, like it's fleeing for its life. Shit! This is exactly how I ended up with Micah. Shit! I scramble off the bed, take a deep breath, and do my best to blow it off. What's the likelihood of me getting pregnant after one time with Jordan? I pull on my dress and slide on my shoes, all while counting out how long it's been since my last period.

"Um. Well, I'm sure…" The words are sticking in my throat, and they won't budge no matter how hard I try to pull them free.

"Reggie," Jordan coos. He slides on his boxers and pins me with his searching gaze. "Don't disappear, okay? I know I screwed up this morning. Forgive me?"

Forgive him? Ha! That's just what I need is to be the mother of two fatherless children. What does he know? *Deep breath.* I guess it's not like we're both not at fault. I didn't say anything about a condom; I wasn't even thinking about it, actually.

"Sure, Jordan. It's no biggie. I'm clean. You know, because—"

"It's been a long time for you, yeah. That's not what I was talking about."

"Oh. Yeah, we're good. We should be good." *Right?* I find my small purse sitting next to my car keys in the kitchen. Jordan follows me to the door, leans down, and presses a featherlight kiss to my lips before I slip out the door.

***

Two days and seventeen texts back and forth from Jordan, and all I can think about is his hands on me, our bodies pressed together, and how amazingly sore I was. Shortly after arriving at work, a massive bouquet of blush-colored roses arrive from Jordan wishing me a happy Valentine's Day. My mind is gushing while I field calls all morning at work, which helps a little to keep my mind off the other *thing* that happened the morning I high-tailed it out of his condo. I've convinced myself that if I don't think about it, nothing will come of it.

I was supposed to take Micah up to visit my parents last Saturday, but we still haven't reconciled after Mom tried to get me to move last month. I'm still upset about how presumptuous my mom was in putting a deposit down on a house for me. But I should call and at least try to work something else out.

"Hello?" Mom's voice trills on the line as though she was expecting a call from one of her best friends.

"Hey, Mom."

"Regina? I wasn't expecting a call from you."

"You have caller ID, Mom. You knew who was calling before you answered."

She sighs, and it's like I can hear the wheels turning in her brain. "We missed you this past weekend."

"Sorry," I say, releasing a sigh of my own. "When can we make it up to you?"

"Your father and I have some business to attend to in Phoenix next weekend. Why don't we come stay with you?"

I grit my teeth and hold back the argument growing. When they stay with me, I end up sleeping on the couch since Stacey and Micah both have their own rooms. But, I might as well agree so we can move past this awkwardness. They are my parents after all, and even though they can drive me crazy, I still love them. They are really good to Micah.

"Sure, Mom. I'll make sure my room is all ready for you."

After a beat of silence, she asks what Micah and I have been up to and somehow, my stupid mouth opens up and spills that I've been seeing Jordan. I can just imagine Mom's shoulders sagging as she flinches at his name.

"You know that boy is nothing but trouble, honey. He's not the kind of guy who will ever stick around or be faithful. You know that, right?"

"We're just having a good time together. I'm not looking for a forever with him."

"You're not sleeping with him, are you?"

I groan into the phone. "Mom! That is none of your business."

"Regina Mariquita Velasco, you already have one fatherless child, you do not need a second. Please tell me you're being careful," Mom says in a hurried ramble, resorting to using my middle name, Mariquita—*Ladybug*.

Careful? The first three times we were. Shit. Now I'm thinking about the thing I don't want to think about again.

"I'm going to hang up now," I say quickly. "I love you, and I'll see you and Dad on Friday."

I end the call, flop my arms on top of my desk, and lay my head down. Where do I see this thing with Jordan going? Can I see it ending in anything but heartache? It hurt so badly when I broke up with him in high school; I seriously couldn't breathe without gasping for air for months. But we were so good together back then. And it feels like a piece of my body I've been missing has returned, and it's great. Perfect, really. Why couldn't we work? I sit up straight and shoot Jordan a text asking when I can see him again.

Jordan: You looking for a replay of Friday night?

Me: Maybe...

I didn't mean to be quite so forward, but what can I say? Just the anticipation of his hands on me again has me squirming in my seat.

Jordan: I'm at sound check all day, but how about tonight? Dinner, my place?

And it's set. Regardless of if what's growing between us is meant to be or not, I'll see him again tonight.

Chapter 21

Jordan

As a band, we haven't done much song collaboration over the past couple years, and I have to say what we're writing is really good. The sound is fresh, and it's flowing from us all. I love writing music sober and never thought it would've been possible, but the music is pure and raw.

The piano was my first love, which some may find a bit unusual. My grandparents had a small upright in their family room, and I was pounding away on the ivory keys at the age of four. By seven I could play most songs I heard—I had an ear for music. I finally started lessons, sped through the books quickly, and ended up outplaying three piano teachers.

I love the simplicity of the black and white keys that hide the complexity under the lid. Strings, pedals, dampers, and hammers are just the beginnings that make up each individual sound. There are eighty-eight keys, and with that, an unlimited number of notes that can then be transformed into music.

I guess in a way a piano is like a woman—touch her just right and she'll sing for you.

All right, I didn't really have to go there, but it got me thinking about Reggie. I'm beginning to wonder if I'm getting in over my head with her. The last thing I want is to go all in like during high school and then have to break her heart when I leave for tour.

Shaking my head to clear my thoughts of her, I return to the piano and the notes spilling from my fingers to the keys. Grant is setting the pace with the drums and when Eddie joins with the guitar, it's magic. Drake comes in on the bass, and I step away from the piano to let Carson take over. He's amazing at reading the chicken scratches I like to call notes. My head bobs to the sound; my eyes close and I feel the music deep inside. And God I feel it. I feel it all.

I feel the memory of Reggie's fingers as they glided across my chest and her warm breath against my neck as she cried out my name. And the *music*, we have it, and as the guys return to the opening notes, I grab the mic and let the words float from my lips. I sing the song as though I'm singing for Reggie and only her. This song may not be directly about her, but as the tempo slows to accommodate the emotion, I feel like every note flies from me, floats across the city, and finds Reggie, wherever she may be, landing on her sun-kissed skin and proclaiming to the world: she's mine.

We head to the diner to break for lunch, and

Reggie texts me to see when we can meet up again, making a smile spread across my face. Apparently I'm not the only one still thinking about Friday night. I want to ask her more, ask if she remembers how my lips felt on her skin or how we couldn't get enough of each other. But I don't because I've had issues all day with my jeans being too tight each time I think about her. I swear it's like I'm a horny teenager in high school again. Except I don't think I was quite this bad back then.

I make a mental note to ask Reggie since she would probably remember best.

Jeremy and I stay at the diner while the other guys take off to grab us some more water for sound check. He's been unusually quiet all day, and now he's not looking at anything except his fingers, which keep balling into fists.

"Spill it, JD. What's eating at you?" I ask. He sighs, clenches his fists tighter, and I know something is definitely up.

"She's pregnant." Something in my chest cracks open and falls to my knees.

"She can't be pregnant, dude. We just had sex last Friday."

Jeremy glances up at me; his eyes are narrowed in confusion.

"Not Reggie. Emily." He puffs out his cheeks and turns his gaze back to his hands. Emily? *Emily.* Oh shit.

"Are you sure? I mean, how do you know it's yours?" I don't mean to sound like an asshole, but he doesn't even know this chick. It's been almost three weeks since he's seen her, can you really know you're pregnant so soon?

"Dude," he says, shaking his head. "Don't be a jerk. She broke up with her boyfriend two months before we hooked up, and I'm the only one she's been with since."

"She says that, but how do you really know?" I'm sitting here in the booth trying to picture a miniature JD running around, and I guess out of all of us, he's the one I can see settling down. But with a chick he hardly knows?

"I don't feel right about demanding a paternity test at this point, so I'm choosing to believe her. Why would she lie about it?"

"One," I begin, raising my fingers to make my point, "money. Two, you manage White Shadow. Three, fame. Four, money. Shall I go on?"

Jeremy's face pales, and his eyes widen as if he hasn't thought about this. I love this guy, and he'd give the shirt off his back in the dead of winter to someone who needed it, but I'm worried he's getting screwed. This chick is possibly only after him for his connections, and I don't want to see my best friend hurt.

"What are you going to do?" I ask.

"I don't know yet. I'm still trying to wrap my head around the whole thing."

"Didn't you put a glove on it?"

He sits upright, shrugs, and then drags his hands over his face. "I wasn't prepared, dude. I'm not usually the one hooking up with girls." He glances knowingly at me, and damn it hurts a little. I don't need to be told how much I've screwed up my life sleeping with dozens of girls over the years.

"How's it going with Reggie?" Jeremy asks, changing the subject. "I couldn't help but overhear how well you two were getting along." His mouth quirks into a goofy grin but fades when I crumble up a napkin and throw it at him.

"Asshole," I say, grinning ear to ear like a damn teenager again.

Jeremy laughs, tosses the napkin back at me, then goes for one more dig. "I'm pretty sure our neighbors heard you two getting it on. Made it really hard to hang out with Emily and watch a movie."

Well, that's news. "I didn't know you brought her back to the condo."

Jeremy's cheeks brighten. *Oh.* I see, it wasn't just about hanging out.

"She's already pregnant." He shrugs, finishes his soda, and we both stumble out of the booth laughing. I clap him on the shoulder and give him a brotherly squeeze. He's as close to blood as he can be. JD is my brother in every sense of the word, except DNA.

Chapter 22

Reggie

I will not stay the night at Jordan's house tonight. This has become my mantra ever since we made plans to have dinner again. At his place. I mean, come on. Any girl knows that's code for spare panties, because the ones you arrive in will either be torn apart or possibly lost. But I don't bring a change of clothes.

Because.

I will not stay the night at Jordan's house tonight.

I won't.

I probably won't.

"You look great," Stacey says as she kisses my cheek at the door. For the first time since I've known her, her upbeat pep seems to be fading. And I feel guilty about it.

"Everything okay?" I ask while I check my purse for my wallet, phone, and keys.

She shrugs, offering me a smile I can only

describe as cozy. Stacey's smiles are not normally cozy. They're wide, welcoming, and contagious. This smile is not that.

"Have fun tonight, okay?" She sighs before sitting down on the couch next to Micah. "Just, you know, be careful."

My cheeks burn in embarrassment, which is stupid because I'm twenty-six years old and should feel confident to sleep with whomever I want.

"We're being careful."

Stacey turns back to me with that same cozy smile. "I wasn't talking about..." She mouths the letters S-E-X. If it's not sex she's referring to, then what is it? "Protect your heart. I think you're playing with fire, and I don't want to see you go through the Jordan breakup whirlwind again."

"That won't happen," I say, but then inhale sharply. "I mean, we're just hanging out. There's nothing serious going on between us."

"What you're doing is pretty serious, Reggie, considering there hasn't been anyone since *him*." I cringe at her referral to Micah's father.

"That won't happen again." I quickly kiss Micah and tell him I love him, before giving Stacey a quick hug as well. "Love you both. I'll be home later."

Stacey's comments roll around in my head while I drive to Jordan's condo. Am I protecting my heart? Or am I rushing toward Jordan with blinders on? By the time I'm in the elevator, I've chewed my nails to nothing, and my stomach is growling. At Jordan's door I could probably pass out.

I'm not protecting anything. In fact, I've let my

guard down enough I've totally lost my armor. I'm in love with Jordan Capshaw. Again. Maybe I never fell out of love with him.

Jordan answers the door wearing a hesitant smile and questioning eyes. His arms wrap me in a delicious hug, and I take the opportunity to breathe him in. The unique scent reminds me of summers spent at the lake skinny-dipping or hiding from the sun under the cover of massive boulders.

"So, don't be mad," he says while still hugging me. I glance up at his light brown eyes as he dishes out a devilish grin and then leans close to whisper in my ear. "We have company. JD and Emily are going to hang with us."

We turn and I see Emily sitting at the counter in the kitchen with Jeremy pouring her a glass of water. Happy freaking Valentine's Day to me.

"Hey, Jeremy. Emily," I say, setting my purse on the counter. "Happy Valentine's Day."

Emily smiles, tucks a strand of her blond hair behind her ear, and glances at Jeremy. He smiles awkwardly back, and I'm wondering what they are doing here together. It's obvious neither feels comfortable around the other.

"What's on the menu tonight? Can I help with anything?"

Jordan sits next to me at the counter, scooting close enough to spread his legs around me. His hand pushes my hair over my shoulder, and then he brushes a whisper of a kiss across my jaw. Pretty sure I will never grow tired of him kissing or touching me.

"I ordered in, and it should be arriving—" A

sharp knock at the door interrupts him. "Now." He smiles and leaps off the bar stool. Moments later, he returns to the kitchen holding four white paper bags filled with food from Marillio's, one of Phoenix's best and most expensive Italian restaurants.

The four of us sit at the counter sharing the pastas, vegetables, and bread, not bothering to use plates. I love this side of Jordan. He's carefree, at ease, and he finds some way to touch me throughout the meal. A brush of his fingers over my thigh, or a quick peck on my cheek, little things to keep my body attuned to his. I reciprocate by leaning close, resting my back on his shoulder. The space we occupy is charged with heated friction as we breathe in a synchronized rhythm, and right now I'd give anything to be here with only Jordan.

Instead, the four of us move to the couches and begin to watch a movie, some lighthearted romantic comedy I can't pay attention to. I'm lying against Jordan's chest, between his thighs with a blanket covering us. His hand has been slowly teasing my breasts and has now moved south. My breath hitches as he stealthily pops the button of my jeans and slides his hands down, down, down…

Heat rushes to my cheeks, and I swear there's a fire licking at my chest as his fingers find their destination. He shifts behind me, gaining better access, making it even more difficult for me to keep a stoic face. Jordan's fingers are meant for the piano; they're long, agile, and they feel so good. My fingers curl over his thigh, gripping him hard, begging him to stop—we shouldn't be doing this with Jeremy and Emily in the same room. I can't keep my breathing regular; it's coming in shallow pants while my body heats from core to cheeks. My grip on his thigh tightens, but his fingers speed up, bringing me closer and closer. My hips buck under the blanket, but Jordan pushes them down and kisses my burning neck as I come down from the orgasm. My heart is racing, Jordan's hard length presses against my lower back, and I'm ready for round two.

"Your room. Now," I whisper, fixing my jeans, and then take his hand in mine, while I slide off the couch.

Chapter 23

Jordan

Reggie's hair feels like silk as it glides between my fingers. She's tucked between my arm and chest, head on my shoulder. It gives me full access to her long black hair. A soft snore passes through her lips and it's incredibly cute. She didn't do that in high school, and I'm totally okay with it.

I must have a magical tongue because even though she tried to go home last night, somehow I convinced her to sleep here. Now it's morning, and I have her still in my arms. I don't want her to ever leave. That should scare me, but somehow it's like a weight has been lifted from my chest. Like I've carried around this elephant and it's been stomping on me every day, pushing me down, trying to suffocate me. But with Reggie here, the elephant has morphed into a sparrow and weighs nothing. In fact, it's so light it may as well not be there at all.

Reggie stirs in my arms, and I pull her close then press my lips to her forehead. Hers turn up in a warm smile, and her eyes flutter open. A pink blush forms on her cheeks as her thigh climbs up mine and ultimately stops on my morning wood. I cock my brow, daring her to keep going, but her eyes widen and she jerks upright in bed.

"What time is it?" she says, glancing all over the room.

I place my hand on her bare shoulder and give a quick squeeze. "Hey," I say. When she won't look at me, I pull her chin toward me. "Relax. It's early. You have plenty of time to make it home to get ready for work."

She releases a breath, rolls her shoulders, and then climbs out of bed. She walks—bare ass naked—across the room, pulling a groan from deep in my throat. She is so damn sexy. I'm going to have to take a cold shower after she leaves this morning, because it's obvious she doesn't intend on joining me back in bed. She tugs on her jeans and shirt, covering the breasts I lavished last night. Why is it we wear clothes? I mean, we're given these bodies, shouldn't we be able to admire them whenever we want?

Lyrics!

I leap out of bed, my junk swinging back and forth as I scramble to the dresser where I keep a pen and a pad of paper. I scribble down a few lines, concentrating on the words circling in my head.

"I've got to go," Reggie says from behind me. Her arms circle my chest in a warm hug, and she kisses my shoulder. "Maybe we could go away for a night over the weekend, just you and me?" she suggests as one of her hands trails down my stomach and covers my half-mast, which springs to life at her touch. The pen stills on the notepad as she pumps and squeezes me.

"Reggie-bug," I warn, but she doesn't relent. Instead, her lips glide across the skin on my back, making me groan and rock my hips into her skilled hand. "Three…two…one," I say as she milks me dry, followed by a quick kiss on my lips.

"Just a little something to think about when I'm not here," she says, and saunters into the adjoined bathroom to wash up. Hell yeah, I'll be thinking about her. She rushes out of the bathroom, plants a firm kiss on my cheek, and leaves in a hurry, taking with her some of the joy I felt earlier.

When I finally emerge from my bedroom, Jeremy is cooking breakfast for himself and Emily, who is wearing his shirt from last night. She's sitting at the counter reading a book and tapping her foot to some song she must have in her head.

"Morning," I say, pulling the orange juice from the fridge and pouring some into a glass. Jeremy tips his head, and Emily shyly says hi, her cheeks blushing as she dives back into reading. *Okay*. I stand next to JD and ask, "Is she always this awkward?"

He stops scraping the eggs from the pan and gives me a pointed look. "She's not awkward. She's just a little starstruck by you," he whispers, and returns to his eggs. Ah, well, I can understand that, though I hate the thought of people being nervous around me. I never wanted to be that guy who made other people uncomfortable.

"You want some of this?" Jeremy asks, pointing

147

to the eggs and bacon. If he's cooking, then I'm definitely eating. I nod enthusiastically and join Emily at the counter. The color of her cheeks darken as I pull the book away from her and flip to the cover.

"You always bring romance novels wherever you go?" I ask, pushing it back to her. Jeremy's eyes narrow at me, but I choose to ignore him.

"Actually, yes, I do. But this one isn't a romance novel, despite the cover. It's historical fiction."

"About a big-busted woman wearing a pearl necklace?"

Emily dog-ears her page and closes the book, then proceeds to read the back of the novel to me. Okay, so it's about a ballerina and the hardships she faced in the early 1900s.

"Fine. It's not a romance. But you do bring a book wherever you go?"

She nods and says, "You never know when you need to pass some time."

We go back and forth until Jeremy slaps two plates on the counter and tells us to eat. He glares at me while leaning over his breakfast.

Emily seems nice. Even though I thought she was after something other than Jeremy, she seems legit. And JD seems happy, even with the pregnancy news. Still, if they're still together when she has the baby, I'll encourage him to have a DNA test done.

When they leave the condo, I grab a quick shower and sit down at the piano with my notepad. When I write songs, the lyrics spill out of me first and the notes flow easily when attached to the right words. Hours later, my stomach growls, the sun has set, and I'm still alone in the condo. I grab a quick sandwich and sit on the couch to watch some television, giving myself a much needed break from the firm piano bench.

An incoming text wakes me up, though I didn't realize I had dozed off. I sit up, turn off the TV, and glance around the condo. It's after eleven, and Jeremy is still not home. He must be staying with Emily. I check my phone and see it's a message from Reggie asking if I'd thought about going away this weekend. I respond with a resounding yes!

Reggie: Yay! Where should we go?

Me: Sedona?

Reggie: Perfect!

I strip out of my clothes, lie down in the bed, which smells like Reggie, and ball my hands into fists before slamming them on the mattress. I want her lying next to me. I want to hear her soft breathing and wake up every morning with her head on my shoulder. Damn, I really miss the girl.

Being with her in high school was easy, not that she didn't make me work at our relationship. It was just something that felt right, like she moved to Phoenix with her family just to be with me. Like somehow the universe pushed us together, and we fit like peanut butter and jelly. We did everything together, and when we broke up it crushed me—I just never saw it coming. I think a part of me used

149

that hurt to fuel my addiction. When the guys and I went on tour and started partying and doing drugs, it was like I could hide from the pain. The drugs numbed me, and I eventually forgot about it. I forgot I used to find myself picking up the phone to call her and tell her about the show we just performed or how we finally landed the contract to headline our own tours. My life was in a constant state of forgetting Reggie.

Now forgetting her is the last thing I want.

I want to remember the four freckles on her left shoulder and how it looks like an artist painted them on in a short, straight line. I want to remember the hollow in her neck and how it deepens when I kiss her. I want to remember how holding her in my arms feels like home and hope and promises.

But I'm leaving in two months for a six-month tour. I won't have her with me. I won't be able to hold her in my arms and breathe in her floral scent. Knowing this, it feels like a dull knife wedges itself between my ribs and tries to steal my breath. A pain grips me when I think about leaving her.

How am I ever going to leave her?

I know it's late, but Washington is an hour earlier than Phoenix this time of year, so I dial up Jemma, hoping she'll be able to knock some sense into me.

"Jordan, are you okay?" I hate that every time I call her she feels the need to make sure I'm not doing something to screw up my life.

"It's nice to hear your voice too," I say, mildly irritated.

"I'm sorry. It's just late, and last time you

called—"

I cut her off, knowing last time I called I was so desperate for help only she has been able to give me.

"Yeah, I'm good. Great actually." We talk for some time about Roger and how he's been there for me. Then she talks about how she and Vic are slowly setting up the nursery in the house Vic built. After Gran died and they got married, Jemma decided to sell the house and land, because it hurt too much living there without her grandmother. What she doesn't know is that I bought it. I had my lawyers draw up an offer and send it anonymously, and thankfully she accepted. I'm the proud owner of forty acres, an old house, and an even older barn— with a Jordan-size, fist-shaped hole in the wall.

"Glad to hear it, Jordan. Sounds like you're doing well." I hear Vic in the background offer a greeting. "Vic says hi."

"Yeah, I got that. So." There's no way to get this out other than just spilling it, so here goes. "I'm kind of seeing someone, and I don't know what to do about going on tour in a couple months."

The line is silent, and for a second I think the call was dropped. "Jemma?"

"I'm still here," she says. "I guess I don't know what to say. I'm happy you've found someone. You want to tell me about her?"

I do so much. And it pours from me and Jemma listens as our story is told, from the first time Reggie and I met in high school all the way to the end of our relationship. How the drugs not only grabbed hold of me but how they started out as a

151

way to numb the pain. I keep going until she's all caught up, and my fears of losing Reggie when I go back on tour are laid out like cards on a table.

"Are you in love with her?" she asks when the words stop flowing and silence fills the air.

"No," I say much too quickly.

Wait.

"I don't know. Maybe?"

I've just spent the last forty minutes telling Jemma about Reggie and how she makes me feel. Could it be that I *do* love her? I look forward to seeing her whether on a date or not, knowing I want to make her smile every second of every day. She makes me want to be a better man even though I'm not worthy of her. I want to prove myself to her, show her I can be who she needs. Several years have passed since high school, but we're somehow able to pick right up where we left off. Being with her is like breathing. I can't live without her.

Shit.

"Jordan," Jemma warns.

Shit. Did I say that out loud?

"Sorry," I say, clamping my eyes closed and squeezing the bridge of my nose. "I freaking love her, and that scares the sh—crap out of me."

Jemma laughs on the other end of the call and tells me to breathe. As if that is going to fix this problem.

"It's not funny, Jemma." Great, Vic is in the background laughing as well. Why do they think me being in love with Reggie is funny? Am I that unlovable? Do they think I'm not good enough for someone to love me?

"I'm sorry," she says. "It's not that I'm laughing at you. I just think it's funny you're scared."

"I'm so glad I can be your source of entertainment for the night."

"If you love her, tell her. If the two of you are meant to be, you'll both figure it out." Jemma's advice is solid, but it doesn't help. The issue at hand is I don't know if I can go on tour knowing I'm leaving behind the woman I love. Shit, it feels strange to say that.

"Jordan, if she loves you too, it will all work out. I promise."

How can she promise this when I can't even admit to myself how I truly feel about Reggie?

Chapter 24

Reggie

Stacey is being very vague about where she's going to be this weekend. In fact, other than telling me my parents will have Micah all to themselves, she's said nothing about her plans. We never keep secrets, so what is she hiding from me? Micah's in bed for the night, and she's in her room, packing. Now's as good a time as any to confront her.

I knock three times on her bedroom door and press my ear to the cold wood. On the other side, I hear the rustling of clothing and Stacey muttering a soft curse. Has our friendship really grown into this weird place where we have to hide things from each other?

The door swings open, and Stacey peeks out from the other side. "Hey, what's up?"

"Can I come in?" I ask, since she hasn't offered yet. And by offered, I mean she hasn't opened the door more than six inches. Stacey's eyes dart to the left and then back to me before she closes them and swings the door open the rest of the way.

"Is something wrong? I feel like you're hiding things from me." I sit on the edge of her bed and think back to when we first moved in together after high school. We'd been best friends since I moved to Phoenix, but becoming roommates was one of the best things in my life. I needed her then, and she was there for me. Now, sitting here glancing around her room, I see barely any traces of my eighteen-year-old best friend. Where her room used to be shades of violet and cream, now they're the more subdued colors of a fashionable adult—beige and white. Her posters of teenage rock bands have been replaced with artwork she's collected through the years. When did she grow up? When did *I* grow up?

Stacey pulls her suitcase off her bed and sits down next to me. She sighs and my heart threatens to fall to the floor. *I'm losing my best friend.*

"Reggie, you know I love you," she says as her arm snakes over my shoulder. This can't be good. It's almost like the dreaded "it's not you, it's me" talk.

"But?" I ask, now totally unsure I want to know what's going on.

She sighs again and says, "I'm having a really hard time watching you go out with Jordan. I remember how you were after you broke up with him, and I don't want to see that happen again."

We've had this talk before, recently, and I feel justified in calling bullshit. Her secrecy can't be because of me and Jordan dating.

"Then why does it feel like you're hiding from me and keeping secrets? I can't imagine that has anything to do with Jordan."

"Micah's been asking questions, Reggie. He's almost eight years old; he's not stupid. He knows something is up, and it's breaking his heart when you're not here and I can't tell him where you are. Don't you think it's time you talked to him about his father?"

"You know I can't do that." I can't sit still with the way my stomach is rolling over and over. The need to pace overwhelms me.

"Why not? If not now, then when? One of these days your sweet little boy will find out where you sneak off to, and it's going to crush him." Stacey bites her lip and stares at me while I pace. It does nothing for the nerves in my stomach.

"I don't know, okay? Is that what you want to hear? That I'm selfish and want to give Jordan another chance? That when I'm with him sometimes I forget I have a son at home waiting for me? Okay then, there you have it. My son's father knows nothing about him, and I don't have any idea how to tell him because if I do, I'll lose him. And then what?"

I slump to the floor and shove the heels of my hands into my eyes as tears roll down my cheeks. What am I doing? I've never yelled at Stacey like this, and I'm getting ready to go on an overnight trip with Jordan. I must have lost my mind the night Jordan stepped into Eggceptional. Stacey's sitting next to me in a heartbeat, her arm pulling me in for a comforting hug. She brushes the hair off my forehead and squeezes me closer.

"I don't think you're being selfish," she says

calmly. "I just want you to really think about how much time you're spending with Jordan and what this could mean for Micah. He needs to know, Reggie. They both deserve to know."

When I've composed myself enough to speak again, I pull my friend in for a real hug and sniff the ugly cry away. Maybe this weekend I can use the time with Jordan to tell him about Micah. Stacey's right; the boys in my life need to know about each other.

"So are you going to tell me where you're sneaking off to this weekend?" I ask as Stacey pulls me to my feet. Her cheeks flush, and I know. It's a boy; it has to be.

"Who is he? Do I know him?" In all the years we've lived together, Stacey's been respectful to the point of living like a nun when at home. She's never brought a guy over because she didn't want to confuse Micah—all of her sexcapades took place somewhere else. And I love her for it. But she's never gone AWOL for a weekend. An overnighter here and there, sure, but the whole weekend? This guy must be something.

"No, you don't know him, but he's great. His name is Ike, and he's an MMA fighter."

Wait, what? "He's a what? A fighter? Isn't that dangerous?"

"He's fighting this weekend in Vegas, and I'm going with him."

My beautiful friend has stars in her eyes, and I suddenly want to meet this guy to make sure he's good enough for her. What if he has a temper and takes it out on my best friend?

157

"How did you meet him?" What I really mean to ask is when did she have time to meet him? She's always picking up the slack from me when I'm working.

Stacey laughs and bats her eyes. "I do have a life outside of Reggie's world, you know."

"I know, but a fighter? Couldn't you have met a boring accountant? At least someone less—"

"Less what?" Her hands are folded across her chest, and her lips twist into a scowl. I've struck a nerve.

"Less violent. What if he hits you? He fights people for a living, Stacey. Hitting someone because they're angry isn't uncommon for people like him."

"And you're basing this on what, experience?" She tosses her suitcase back on her bed and throws open the top flap. "Because last I checked, you haven't dated anyone seriously since Jordan, and now that you're riding that train again I think you should just butt out of my love life."

My jaw falls open, and I'm completely at a loss for words. What just happened? I stand in the middle of the room as she continues to pack, tossing in bits of clothing here and there, obviously not caring how it goes in the suitcase. She steps around me each time she needs to grab something from her dresser, but remains silent. I have no idea how to fix this rift growing between us.

"Mommy?" I turn to see Micah wiping his tired eyes with the backs of his fists. His brown hair is sticking up in odd places, and his cheeks are flushed from sleep. I rush over to him, swipe my hand over his forehead to check for a fever, but there is none.

"What's wrong, buddy?" I ask as I wrap my arms around him in a hug. Mommy needs a hug right now, really badly. He clings to me, wraps his legs around my waist, and lets me carry him back to bed. One day, probably sooner than I'll like, this little boy is going to be too heavy for me to lift, and it's going to make me so stinking sad.

"Are you okay?" I ask, tucking him into bed.

He nods sleepily and yawns. "Why were you and Auntie Stacey fighting?" I wince. I hadn't realized we were so loud.

"It's nothing, buddy. Go back to sleep, and I'll see you in the morning, okay?" I place a kiss on his forehead and watch him turn to his side and easily fall back asleep. I sit with him for a while longer and remember the day I first held him in my arms. He was a tiny little thing, just under seven pounds. I was so scared I was going to break him, and the nights where he cried and cried just about killed me. Thank goodness for Stacey, who's been with me every step of the way and has always had my back. She was there when my parents wanted nothing to do with me after I told them I was pregnant. And she held my hand in the delivery room and changed his diapers when I was too exhausted to do it.

I have to apologize to her before something happens and our friendship is ruined.

I kiss Micah's forehead once again, leave his room, and step across the hall to Stacey's. I don't knock this time. Instead, I let myself in and walk right over to her and wrap her in a hug.

"I'm sorry I've been a jerk lately," I say when I

move away. We both laugh, hug again, and make our apologies. When all the air is cleared, I help her finish packing. We sit up eating Tonight Dough from Ben & Jerry's and gush about the men in our lives just like high school.

***

Stacey left early this morning, and my parents are set to arrive any minute. I've been running around like crazy today, and I hope the house is clean enough for them. Mom is really good at pointing out the dust on the picture frames or an un-fluffed pillow, so the less ammunition the better. And just like that, there's a knock on the door, and I look like I've been cleaning all day. Perfect.

"Mom! Dad!" I gush when I open the door. Mom glances around the room with a practiced smile and hands me her purse and jacket. Dad makes his way back to Micah, who's running down the hall with his arms outstretched, awaiting the bear hug he'll get.

"There's my boy," Mom says with a real smile. She joins Dad in a group hug, and I'm left hanging her coat and purse on the hooks by the door, watching them feed my son with attention. Don't get me wrong, I'm very grateful they love him; I just miss the love they once showed me. I suppose it was lost when I got pregnant and wasn't married.

We eat a simple dinner of tacos and then sit and play a game with Micah until his bedtime. Dad puts him to bed and joins me and Mom on the couch. Why do I feel like I'm about to be lectured again?

This is all too familiar, and so I stand up, reach for the remote, and quickly turn on the TV, choosing a show I know they both enjoy. We sit in heavenly silence while the show is on and, thankfully, I receive a text from Jordan to distract me.

Jordan: You ready for the weekend?

Me: Can it start right now?

Jordan: Sure! Come on over.

I could go to his place tonight, but it would give my parents yet another thing to dislike about me and Jordan dating again.

Me: I can't. Don't want to risk the wrath of Mom.

Jordan: That's some scary shit right there!

Jordan: Call me later?

Me: Okay.

My parents are already yawning and it's only nine. They stand, and Dad stretches while Mom yawns again.

"Good night, Regina," Mom says with yet another practiced smile. I wonder if she's always smiled like that and I never noticed it growing up. Maybe that's the only smile she has. No, that's wrong. The one she gives Micah is wide and welcoming, and I have faint memories of receiving it when I was younger.

"I'll see you in the morning." They make their way to my bedroom and close the door. They'll hopefully be in there the rest of the night, giving me the lumpy couch all to myself. Not that I couldn't sneak into Stacey's bed and sleep in hers, but she didn't offer and I didn't ask. I scroll through the TV channels and stop on a movie I've been wanting to watch, then call Jordan.

"Hey, Bug." His low voice makes my skin erupt in goose bumps. "Whatcha doing?"

"I just turned on a movie. Want to watch it with me?"

"Are you inviting me over?" He fakes a gasp, making me laugh.

"No. Turn to channel 264, and we can watch it together. Like a long distance date."

"Is there any sex in this movie?"

Maybe I should invite him over just so I can throw a pillow at him.

"Just watch it with me. We can stay on the phone during the movie, and it'll be like we're in the same room," I say. I settle into the couch, pull a blanket over my legs, and push the pillows under my head. Perfect.

"But there won't be any touching during this movie," he says with a pout. "You know how much I like to touch you."

"Shhh. Just watch the movie." And we do. By the end I'm a blubbering mess when the female lead dies in the arms of her lover. "What kind of movie was that?" I ask, wanting to get Jordan's opinion about the rotten ending. But he doesn't answer me. I hold the phone up to my ear and hear faint snoring.

"Jordan?" Still, he doesn't answer. "Good night, Jordan," I whisper as I hang up the phone.

Chapter 25

Jordan

"That movie was lame," I say as Reggie and I pull away from the condo. "And you know it."

"How would you know? You fell asleep watching it."

"I did not." I totally did. I don't think I made it twenty minutes before I fell asleep.

"You were so sleeping. I heard you snoring."

"I don't snore." Sometimes I do.

"Whatever." Reggie folds her arms across her chest in a mock-pout, giving me the urge to reach over and poke her ribs. She's incredibly ticklish there. She jumps when I poke my finger in her side, squeals, and slaps my hand away. She looks beautiful this morning with the sun shining on her hair as we drive north on the I-17 toward Sedona. I've reserved a room at a fancy bed and breakfast that backs up to a stream. The room looked perfect on the website, with its log-like walls and river rock fireplace.

I thread my fingers through hers as we drive and marvel at the woman sitting next to me. I love her and it kills me that I let her walk away from me all those years ago. I was a dumb kid and didn't know I could've fought to keep her. But I have her now, and I don't plan on giving her up ever again.

Whoa.

That's a revelation if I ever had one. I give her hand a quick squeeze and concentrate on the drive ahead.

We pull into the B and B just after eleven, check in with the nice couple who owns the property, and go to our cabin. The outside is a mix of rustic logs and stone surrounded by leafy shrubs. I unlock the door, show Reggie through the threshold, and await her response. Her eyes go wide as she scans the room, and even I have to admit it's really nice. The pictures don't do the cabin justice. We enter a cozy living room where the windows overlook the trees and stream in the back. The stone fireplace is massive, taking up almost an entire wall.

Reggie turns to me, wraps her arms around my neck, and squeals. My heart jumps at her approval and I can't hold back the smile taking over my face. Jordan Capshaw nailed this one!

"Let's go find the bedroom," Reggie says, smiling wide and dragging me through the living room. We pass the kitchen with its dark granite counters and black appliances, but turn around when we find the laundry room. She drags me back through the kitchen and living room to another set of doors.

"Here we are," she says with a sultry smile. She

backs into the room, tugging me by the top of my jeans. Her fingers skim over my stomach. My muscles tighten and, as much as I'd love to get naked with her right here, we have a schedule to stick to. I back away from her touch, and she pushes her lips into a cute little pout.

"We need to grab our swimsuits and head up to the main house for our massages," I say, hoping to pacify my girl. We'll be using the heated pool after the massage. She squeals yet again, only this time she jumps up and down like a hyper puppy trying to snatch a treat.

"You're the best," she says, wrapping me in another warm embrace, though she follows this one with a slow kiss. Her lips move across mine, and when her tongue enters my mouth I grasp her waist and pull her close, groaning that I scheduled these massages. I'm not against cancelling and losing the costs of two massages, but my girl deserves to be pampered.

My hands trail down her hips and stop at her round ass, giving those luscious cheeks a firm squeeze.

"All right, Bug, we need to get going."

Her tongue thrusts into my mouth again before she breaks away. "You sure?"

I back away, scrub my hands over my face, and almost give in. "Come on, let's go." I place a quick peck on her cheek, grab my trunks, and try to keep myself under control as Reggie digs through her suitcase and pulls out something that barely resembles a swimsuit.

"Damn, you gonna wear that for me?"

Her cheeks flush as she pulls the suit to her chest and drags me out of the bedroom and up to the main house. Inside, Margot, one of the owners, greets us and shows us to the changing rooms. There are two rooms—one for men, the other for women—and when Margot leaves us, Reggie saunters inside the women's room. I stand outside, contemplating being a good little boy, but the devil on my shoulder wins and I glance around to see if anyone's nearby before heading into the room with Reggie. I plan on driving her crazy while we're here, and I might as well get started now.

There are two rows of lockers, and I find her at the back row with her jeans already off, puddled around her ankles. She's wearing a lacy black thong and the pink and cream plaid button-down shirt she wore up here, and she's damn beautiful.

"Jordan!" she whisper-screams at me. "You're not supposed to be in here." She backs up and sits down on the bench behind her, staring up at me.

"As far as I can tell, we have the place to ourselves. And Margot never specifically said I can't be in here." I move right in front of her, push her knees apart with my legs, and fall to my knees. Her thighs alight in goose bumps while I run my hands from her knees to the juncture at her hips.

"What are you doing?" she asks breathlessly.

"Making you want me as much as I want you." My thumbs move over the front of her thong, and her entire body straightens, pushing her chest front and center, right in my line of sight—too bad her shirt is covering her. Trailing my lips across her neck and to her waiting lips drives me crazy. Her mouth parts and accepts my tongue, but I refuse to rush this. I move with her slowly, teasing and tempting, but when she pushes for more, I pull away. She whimpers when I stand and reach my hands behind my head to shuck off my shirt. Her eyes rake over my chest as her cheeks flush a bright pink. When she reaches to help me out of my jeans, I move out of her reach, teasing her some more.

"Uh-uh," I tease, popping the button to slowly guide the zipper down. Her eyes follow my fingers and then my jeans as I slide them down my legs. Her lips quirk into a crooked smile and when her hands reach for the top of my boxers, I step back and turn around.

She smacks my butt and yanks the boxers down. "You are such an ass," she says with a laugh, and then throws me a robe.

"What's that you say? I have a nice ass?" I shrug on the robe, tie the terry cloth belt around my waist, and turn just in time to catch a glimpse of Reggie's bare breasts. A lump forms in my throat when I try to think of anything but her naked and under me.

Reggie smirks, dons her robe, and says, "Payback's a bitch, isn't it?"

I quickly store our belongings in the lockers before she rushes out the door to the waiting room. I follow, seriously reconsidering this couple's massage simply because I'll have to lie across from Reggie and listen to the sounds she makes. Tell me how this is not going to end up with me in a compromising position.

Margot brings us to the massage room and introduces us to our masseuses, Nikki and Amber.

Nikki is wearing a black tank top that makes her arms look like a Mack truck; I'm pretty sure she could bench press me.

"This table for you, *da*?" Ah, Russian. "Lie down on your stomachs and cover with the sheet. We'll return shortly. Any questions?" Reggie and I shake our heads in unison and hold back our laughter until the two women leave the room.

"What in the heck is she?" Reggie giggles, covering her mouth with the back of her hand.

"I'm guessing she's a female MMA fighter. Maybe a dude in disguise?" That sets Reggie off, laughter spilling through the gaps of her fingers and warming my chest. I quickly span the room, place my palms on her cheeks, and press her lips to mine. This girl, even her laugh does it for me. She sighs into my lips, parting hers, giving my tongue access to what it craves. As quickly as I initiate the kiss, I pull away, ignoring Reggie's whine of protest.

The massages are amazing. Nikki's hands work the knots from my back and shoulders, making me groan even more than Reggie. After an hour, Nikki and Amber finish our massages and leave us alone in the dim room filled with the scent of lavender and sandalwood. I'm so relaxed I could probably sleep like this and wake up a happy man.

But then I hear the creak of Reggie's massage table as she works her way off of it. Not gonna lie, I stare like a boy looking out the window hoping to see Santa. Her body is flushed from the massage, she has a ring around her face from the hole in the table, and her smile is one I want to memorize. It's a broad, no teeth grin that reaches her eyes, giving

169

her a totally relaxed and satisfied look.

"Quit looking at me like you want to devour me," she teases as she threads her arms through the robe. "You going to get up?"

A laugh leaps from my chest, earning me a look of annoyance. "I'm halfway there," I say, propping myself up on my elbows. "Why don't you come on over here and help me up the rest of the way." Reggie's cheeks light up as she moves closer, only to smack my shoulder and dash out the door.

Back in the changing room, we pull on our swimsuits and walk hand in hand through the building to the heated pool. Late February in Sedona is still pretty chilly, and as soon as we hit the outdoors Reggie shrieks and runs to the steamy water. She tosses her towel near the edge of the pool and leaps off the deck into the blue water, landing with a splash. Shaking my head, I reach down and pick her towel up off the floor and toss it, along with mine, onto a chair near the edge. I really don't want to dry off with a nearly frozen towel sitting on the deck in puddles of pool water.

The pool is meant to look like a lagoon, with the plants surrounding the edges and boulders built in to parts of the pool walls. At the far end is a large rock surface with a waterfall you can swim under. My arms arc over my head as I dive into the warm water. The temperature isn't quite bathwater, but it's close, and feels incredible on my knot-free muscles. I swim under the surface until I reach Reggie, and then I pop out of the water in front of her. She squeals when I pull her under and press my lips to hers.

Chapter 26

Reggie

Everyone should go swimming in a heated pool after a full body massage. It relaxes your muscles even more than they already are, and when paired with Jordan Capshaw, let's just say I plan on somehow making this a regular event. As we swim under the waterfall, Jordan pulls me to his chest and guides me to a seat that blocks us from any intruder's view. He stands between my legs, his hands on the bench seat on either side of my thighs, and his gaze locks on my eyes. His breathing is labored, and my heart rate spikes.

I know this look in his eyes, the hooded gaze with dilated pupils. I know what he wants, but I don't know how far he's willing to go to get it. My fingers glide over his sculpted shoulders, down his arms, and rest on the ledge where I'm sitting. His lips twitch as we draw closer. Our foreheads nearly touch, the tips of our noses only a hair's breadth apart, and neither one of us moving to close the miniscule gap. His breath floats onto my lips, teasing like a dandelion puff, and my eyes close involuntarily. Our skin doesn't touch, but this feels strangely more intimate than anything we've ever done before. It's like an intense form of foreplay, leaving both of us breathless and so hungry for what's to come.

We touch without so much as a brush of skin, but this non-touch is so much more. So much better, like the anticipation of Christmas morning, just knowing I'll get to unwrap him later. If I weren't sitting, totally encompassed by him, my legs would have trouble holding my weight. I am a ball of hungry nerves, frazzled, zapping at our nearness, and fighting the urge to break this tension.

"Reggie-bug." Jordan's breath escapes in the form of my name. The nickname he gave me so many years ago, the one I tried desperately to forget. The one I want to hear spilling from his lips for the rest of my life.

Jordan's lips brush against mine, and my eyes flutter open as I inhale the kiss he's offering. His mouth is like a caress; it's giving and allowing something greater to grow between us. There's no burning fire to douse, no intense hunger or lingering desire to strip our swimsuits off and make the water around us stir like rapids in a river. There's just love. I feel it deep in the pit of my stomach. I feel it in the way each kiss is like a question, like he's asking me if I love him as much as he loves me. The words aren't spoken; right now they don't need to be, because I *feel* them. And that hits me like a giant bag of bricks.

I can't continue to keep Micah a secret. I should never have *kept* him a secret.

My hands push against Jordan's chest, breaking the best kiss I've ever experienced. His head cocks to the side as he quirks his lips into an uneven grin.

"Come on," he says while taking my hand from his chest. "Let's get ready for lunch."

Yes. Lunch will be a good distraction. Maybe I'll come up with the right way to tell him the truth.

After we've both showered and dressed in the room, we drive into Sedona and stop at an eclectic set of orange adobe-stucco buildings. We've come for the Mexican food, but as we walk by the little shops I demand a shopping trip after we've eaten.

Inside the restaurant, we're immediately greeted with the scent of tangy limes, sizzling fajitas, and fresh salsa. It makes my mouth water and my stomach growl just thinking about the food I'll be inhaling soon. We're seated near a water feature in the center of the large room, which is unique in that there are several large koi swimming in the shallow indoor pond.

"This place is amazing," I say between bites of amazing tortilla chips and salsa. The spice and tang of the tomatoes is addicting.

"What are you going to have?" Jordan asks as he folds his menu on the table.

"The filet fajitas, they sound amazing." I smile just thinking about my lunch. "How about you?"

"Carne Asada burrito," he answers quickly. "I pretty much order it wherever I go. I like to keep track of my favorites so when I'm on the road I know where I want to eat."

Bricks to head, stomach falling to my knees. Again. It's like somehow we're in this bubble, and no one around us knows Jordan is the lead singer of White Shadow, one of the most popular rock bands in the U.S. And in this bubble, I can pretend he's all mine, and we can live this perfect, happy life like two normal people.

But we're not in a magic bubble. And there never will be normal for us. Not if he continues his music career.

"You okay?" Jordan asks as he reaches across the small table, threading his fingers through mine. "You seem distracted."

I want to laugh, blow it off and tell him everything is fine. Better than fine. Good, in fact. But it really isn't good. Or fine. I'm kind of going back to freaking out a little. But I can lie. I can pretend I'm good, that we're an average couple spending time together in a beautiful restaurant in gorgeous Sedona. I can pretend for another thirty-six hours that I don't have a son at home who knows nothing about this man I'm with. I can pretend everything is fine.

I smile, grip his hand, and make myself believe this lie. "I'm having the best time with you."

After lunch we visit the little boutique shops near the restaurant. Our hands are linked as we wander the small spaces, admiring the sculptures and touristy t-shirts. At one store I can't resist a prickly pear hand lotion, and I buy three small tubs of it. Jordan laughs as the teenage girl behind the counter focuses on the lotion while placing it in the bag. Her cheeks are bright red, and judging by her initial reaction when we walked through the shop's door, she recognized him. At least she isn't throwing herself at him.

Next on the agenda is a Pink Jeep Tour through the red rocks. I've never been but have heard it's something everyone should experience at least once in their lives. We head to uptown Sedona, meet our driving specialist, Keith, and prepare for the tour. Keith is a twenty-something, long-haired, tanned guy who looks like he belongs on the beaches carrying a surf board. He explains the tour, and Jordan and I hop in the back of the 4x4 Pink Jeep and buckle in.

The landscape is so different from Phoenix— deep red rocks strategically placed one on top of the other, or maybe leftovers from lava slides that cooled in jagged layers. The cacti and other desert plants give almost an herbal scent to the fresh air. We stop off at the first scenic sight, Submarine Rock, climb a little, and take in the site around us. I feel like I've stepped onto another planet, Mars maybe. It's breathtaking, and I snap a few photos with my cell phone camera.

Jordan steps behind me, wraps his arms around my waist, and drags his lips over the shell of my ear. Goose bumps alight on my skin as I shiver against him.

"Having a good time?" he asks, snapping another picture. I nod, and then Keith calls to us, beckoning us back to the Jeep. We make our way through the well-worn Jeep trail, and I squeal at the lurching of the Jeep a couple times. At one point, when the Jeep appears to be heading down a forty-five degree angle, I squeeze my eyes closed and pray the Jeep doesn't flip end over end on the way down the rugged trail. Jordan's laughing and urging me to open my eyes the entire way down the path, but I keep them firmly shut. There's no way I want to witness my death if it comes by way of a Pink Jeep Tour.

"That wasn't so bad," Jordan says as his arm wraps around my shoulders when we're back in uptown Sedona. I tense at his touch, but relax into his warmth, knowing I'm finally safe and back on solid, smooth ground.

"Yeah. I've gone once and never have to go again," I mutter.

Keith beams back at us and assures me this is the only off-road tour; the others are much tamer. I ball up my fist and punch Jordan in his bicep, meeting hard muscle. He feigns injury and then jabs his fingertips into my ribs, tickling me.

We grab a quick dinner before heading back to the bed and breakfast where Jordan showers off the dust from our Pink Jeep Tour. Knowing I won't have a chance to talk to Micah later on tonight, I call my mom's cell to talk with him. When he answers the phone, my heart stills at the sound of his young voice.

"Hi, Mom," he says. I can tell he's slightly distracted, because there are long pauses after each tidbit of conversation.

"Are you behaving for Grandma and Grandpa?" I ask as I sit on the corner of the bed with my back turned to the slightly open bathroom door. I try to speak quietly so Jordan won't overhear.

"I wish I was in Flagstaff instead of here at home," he says with an exaggerated sigh.

"Next month we can go visit the chickens and play at Grandma's house."

He sighs again, practically breaking my heart. "There's nothing to do here at home. All Grandpa wants to do is watch the news, and Grandma won't stop cleaning."

What? My place wasn't dirty when they arrived; I made sure of it. My hand clenches around my cell while I try to rein in the bitterness my mother always brings out in me while she tries to run my life. I take a deep breath and skip right over it.

"I'll be back tomorrow, and we'll go out, just you and me, okay?"

"Okay, Mom. I love you."

"I love you too." My heart stutters in my chest at how sad my little boy sounds. Why can't my parents leave well enough alone and spend time with their grandson? They are great up in Flagstaff, but apparently at my house they ignore him.

"Who was that?" My head jerks around so fast to see Jordan wearing only a towel, leaning up against the doorjamb to the bathroom. His eyes are trained on mine, and there's something like hurt in his features, or maybe it's accusation. My jaw drops as I lower my gaze to the phone in my hand. My brain has left the building, people. Think of something, *anything*.

I clear my throat as the blood rushes to my chest and cheeks. "How long were you listening?" Great way to reassure him, Reggie—by the stricken look on his face, he's offended. "It was just Stacey." I throw out a casual laugh, sliding off the bed and walking towards Jordan.

"Do you always tell Stacey you love her?"

Actually, we do—a lot. I nod and then trail my fingers down the plains of his chest then up over his shoulders. "She's feeling a little left out with how much time I'm spending with you."

Jordan grabs my hands and brings them down between us. He dips his head, leaning ever so close, and says with a goofy smirk, "I don't want you telling anyone you love them unless it's me. Got it?"

Yep. Loud and clear. Gulp.

Chapter 27

Jordan

Reggie's asleep next to me after two marathon rounds of sex, and I should be sleeping too. Hell, she wore me out. There were hands everywhere, lips and tongues and…

I turn my head and watch as her eyes flutter in a dream. Yep, she's definitely asleep. Well, damn. I'm apparently ready for round three just thinking about the way her hips rocked into mine.

Instead, I slowly climb out of this bed with its army of blankets and sheets and head into the bathroom. A cold shower is in order. Or maybe a hot one followed by a cold one.

I let the water cascade over my shoulders and down my back as my thoughts drift to the phone conversation I overheard earlier. Who is she going out with when she gets home? Who is she saying "I love you" to? Those words ripped a hole right through my chest, and even though she's in my bed, she felt distant tonight. Like a part of her was wishing she was somewhere else. *With* someone else. What kind of messed up shit is that?

I hit the tiled wall with the fleshy part of my palm, clamp my jaw, and allow a groan of frustration get lost in the cave of my mouth. I don't need to wake her up, not when I'm trying to patch this hole in my body with lavender-scented soap bubbles.

The bathroom light flicks off, temporarily blinding me. The shower curtain rustles, and soft, warm hands wrap around me from behind. I reach up to position the water spray over us both, and turn around into Reggie's arms. My eyes have adjusted to the dim bathroom, allowing me full access to the shape of this perfect body in front of me. She's always been petite and thin, but the years that have passed between us have added some subtle curves. Her hips are slightly fuller, and her breasts a bit larger and not as perky. Even her stomach, which was once flat and taut, has a little bit of meat to it, though still taut. I love the changes. I love that she looks like a woman. I especially love what she's doing with her hands and the bar of soap.

"You were already ready for me," she says, gazing down at her hand and the suds she's lathered over me. She pumps and squeezes, and I can't stop the grumble in the back of my throat from escaping. Her hand feels damn good. Before she can finish me off, I pull away, tear the bar of soap from her hand and lather it up in my hands.

"Let's see how ready you are," I tease as my hands explore her curves. She responds with subtle noises of her own that make all this nearly too much to handle.

"Now, Jordan," she says, turning her back to me.

"Bug, I don't have a condom in here."

Reggie pulls back the shower curtain, reaching for something. Satisfied with what she retrieves, she turns and glances up at me with a wide smile overtaking her face. In her hand is a small, square foil package. "I came prepared," she says, tearing the package open and sheathing me.

She leans toward the wall, bending over just enough, and I'm a goner. Our bodies join like it's the most natural thing in the world. We fit together as though cut from the same piece of wood, like we've been carved into a matching set.

Her hands are splayed in front of her on the wall; mine are greedy and travel her body, looking for the undiscovered places on the way to her heart. Because I want that. I want her heart. Her body. I want her love more than I've ever wanted anything else in this world. She breaks away, separating our bodies, and turns around. Her cheeks are flushed, her eyes so dark it's like I'm gazing into a pool of oil. Her hands reach behind my neck and clasp together as her lips crash into mine.

I pull her body close, lifting her under her legs and carry her to the bed where I can pour out all the love I feel for her. I want her to catch my heart, because it's climbing up my chest, pushing its way through my throat and barreling through my lips onto hers. I hope she's ready, because nothing can stop it. It's there, waiting for her to take it. Waiting for her to accept what I'm offering. I smooth the damp hair from her face, gaze at the woman beneath me on the bed, close my eyes, and give it to her. One. Breath. At. A. Time.

"My heart's waiting on the tip of my tongue for you, Reggie-bug."

Her eyes flicker to mine; she pulls her bottom lip between her teeth as tears begin to line the rim of her lower lids.

"I love you, and I need you to take it, Bug. I need you to hold it close, because I'm not sure I can keep it inside anymore."

Three. That's the number of tears that slip down the sides of Reggie's face before she swipes them away. A sigh slips through her mouth as she brings her lips to mine. Her arms wrap around my neck, and I know my heart is in good hands. This woman has always held my heart in some way.

"I love you too, Jordan. I love you so much sometimes I think I'm crazy. Or that you being here with me again is just a whacked out dream I'll wake up from in the morning." She sighs, squeezing me tighter before releasing me. I move off her, prop up the pillows against the headboard, and pull her between my legs. She relaxes against me, fitting perfectly again like my missing half.

After watching a movie until late in the night, we sleep in until after ten—so much for eating breakfast here at the bed and breakfast. Instead, we shower, dress, and pack up. Within minutes, we're at the main house checking out. Margot greets us with a knowing smile, pats Reggie's hand, and offers a polite smile as she hands me a coupon for my next visit. I'll come back next weekend if I get to spend it with Reggie. I'd come back tomorrow.

We drive up the road and grab a quick bite to eat before heading back to the valley. Our hands are linked together over the center console, and each time Reggie absentmindedly brushes her thumb across the back of my hand I'm reminded she loves me. I gave her my heart, and she took it. It's there on the redness of her cheeks. I did that. I put that blush there, and damn if it doesn't look good on her.

I squeeze her hand and sneak a glance at her once again. She's gazing out her window, slowly bobbing her head to the music playing softly on the radio. Every once in a while her lips move as though she's singing the words, though no sounds spill from her mouth. My focus is back on the road until she breaks the silence.

"I don't want this weekend to end," she says, puffing out a breath.

Instinctively, I veer the car to the right and pull off to the side of the highway. We've only been on the road for about thirty minutes, and I'm right there with her. I don't want our time together to come to an end either.

"What are you doing?" she shrieks at my sudden stop. Three cars whiz by us before I throw open the car door, quickly close it, and jog around to her side. I pull her door open, lean inside to unbuckle her seatbelt, and drag her out. The air is brisk, immediately bringing out the goose bumps on Reggie's arms. "Jordan?"

My hands rest under her jaw as I bring her face to mine. "These lips belong to me and no one else," I say as my thumb traces over her plump bottom lip. She nods, smiles, and then I take what I want. My tongue slips through her lips, earning a satisfied sigh from my girl and several honks from passing cars. But I don't give a damn who sees us making out along the side of the freeway. I'm staking my claim and letting everyone know.

Chapter 28

Reggie

My lips are still tingling when I drive away from Jordan's condo. He kissed me like he needed it to keep breathing. I don't know what happened this weekend; how we went from seeing each other occasionally to saying "I love you." I knew how I felt, but hearing Jordan offering me his heart nearly killed me. Yes, I want it. Yes, I love him. Yes, I'll take it without question.

Except.

Except I lied to him. I didn't tell him about Micah. How could I? I can just imagine how that conversation would go. Or rather how it wouldn't go. He would walk away from us forever, and it would rip me to shreds. And there would be no one left to stitch together the fragments of me.

As I sit in my car outside my apartment, I prepare to put my mom in her place about coming into my home and cleaning it without me being there. I can be strong, I think. One breath in, one

185

breath out. Okay, I can do this. I pull my small suitcase from the backseat, square my shoulders, and walk up the stairs to my place.

"Mommy!" Micah screeches as he runs to me, throwing his arms around my waist. My heart soars at his affection. I bend down, smell his apple-scented hair, and pull him in a tight hug. I've been gone a day and a half, and I missed my boy so much.

"Regina," Mom says as she walks out of the kitchen drying her hands on a towel. Her eyes roam over me, making my cheeks flush. She totally knows Jordan and I had sex, crap! I mean, I guess it was kind of obvious we would with the whole "going out of town" part. I'm a big girl and can do what I want with whom I want, but the scowl on her lips ups the level of guilt I already feel for leaving Micah again so soon.

"Mom," I say, still holding tightly to my little boy. Slowly I stand, releasing Micah and sending him off to play. I glance over to the couch where Dad is dozing with the news on in the background.

"Micah told me he really felt left out while you and Dad were here," I say, exasperated. "And my house was already clean before you arrived. Why did you need to do more cleaning, Mom?"

Her shoulders tense. I've obviously struck a nerve. "You only surface cleaned, Regina. I just took care of the deep cleaning. It was pretty clear you hadn't done any in quite some time."

Is she serious? "So you figured cleaning my house was more important than spending one-on-one time with your grandson?" I fold my arms across my chest and lean against the front door to support myself.

Mom rolls her eyes while she lays the towel over her shoulder. "You're the one who took off to spend time with the man who knocked you up in the first place. Serves you right he didn't stick around. Thankfully you never told him about Micah. Coming here was a bad idea." She huffs a breath from the back of her throat and returns to the kitchen.

"Mom." The word gets stuck in my throat, escaping more like a choking gasp. Tears prick the corners of my eyes, and my body temperature spikes. My dad stirs on the couch; he's either awake and ignoring the fight brewing between me and Mom, or he's more of a sound sleeper than I realized.

Leaving my suitcase beside the door, I force myself to follow Mom into the kitchen. She's scrubbing at something on the counter with the green dishrag. Her cheeks are red, and she keeps sniffing. She's seriously crying? I'm barely keeping it together here, and it's because of her.

"You know why I didn't tell Jordan about Micah. How dare you use that against me." I stand against the fridge, still needing something to hold me up, to stop my body from shaking in anger and hurt. Mom ignores me, focusing more intently on whatever it is she's scrubbing. "You know I'm grateful that you and Dad stayed with Micah. I just don't understand why you can't ignore the fact that apparently my house isn't clean enough for you. Micah loves you and Dad and was really looking forward to spending one-on-one time with you both."

"Well, whose fault is that? You're the one who chose not to bring Micah for a visit." Mom finally turns around, revealing her watery, red eyes. She's trying her best not to let the tears fall.

Incredible. I'm so upset I don't even know what to say. Does she not realize she keeps pushing me away?

"You can't live my life for me, Mom. I'm twenty-six years old and a mother—I think I'm capable of making my own decisions and living with the consequences."

Mom sobs out a laugh that pierces me like an arrow. "You think your son deserves to have a mother who parades around with an addict who can't keep it in his pants? What's he going to think when he learns who his father is, what kind of man he is?"

"He's clean, Mom. Has been for almost two years."

"And you think that makes everything forgivable? You think because he's clean now, something won't set him off in the future and return him to his natural tendencies?" Mom moves away from the spot she was scrubbing and sits down at the table. She leans against the edge and echoes my posture—arms folded tightly across her chest. "One wrong thing is likely to push him over the edge. You must know this."

My mouth gapes as she sits there telling me to expect the worst from the man I love. What kind of person does that make her when she's only willing to see the negative in someone? Does she not have the capacity to have compassion for others?

"Jordan deserves to be given the benefit of the doubt, Mom. He's doing really well and has a great support system in his band and his addiction counselor." I clench my teeth and prepare to say more, but Mom cuts me off.

"You mean the same support system that got him addicted to drugs in the first place? Those are some real great friends he has."

"Lay off her, Abigail," Dad quips from the kitchen doorway. Mom glances up, her eyes scanning from me to him.

"I just don't know why she's wasting her time seeing that man, Daniel. He's not good for her. And he's definitely not good for our grandson." Mom throws her hands in the air and quickly stands from her chair. She breezes past me and pushes her way through Dad, heading to my bedroom.

Dad pats my shoulder, pulls a glass from the cupboard near the fridge, and fills it with water.

"What am I doing so wrong that makes her hate me, Dad?" I ask, unable to keep tears from slipping down my cheeks.

He sighs, places the glass on the counter, and pulls me in for a gentle, fatherly hug. "Your mother doesn't hate you, Reggie. She loves you very much."

What can I do but laugh? "She has a funny way of showing it."

Dad pushes away and stares down at me through his murky brown eyes. His black hair is graying around the temples, but his oval face still holds a youthful quality.

"She's never been really good at showing her love. At least not in a way you've ever responded well to. She's not a hugger—she's a doer. She serves others to show her love, but you've always needed affection, a reassuring hug or a pat on the back. The two of you are very different, but I promise she loves you."

"Then why does she never say it? Why is she always trying to make decisions for me? I'm happy here. Micah and I are doing well, can't she see that?"

Dad's arms encircle me again, and I realize he's right. Mom and I are very different. I search my memories and remember numerous times as a child I went to hug my mom around her middle only to have her gasp and almost take a step back. She'd be stiff as a board and never reciprocate, so eventually I stopped hugging her at all. I think that's where our relationship started to go wrong.

"Your mom just wants to be close to you and Micah. She doesn't get to see you as much as she'd like, and she hoped that by setting up something new, you'd jump on it. I know you're happy here, even she knows it. But she still hopes one day you'll live closer."

I think I could stay wrapped in my dad's warm arms forever; he makes everything better. I wonder if that's a gift reserved only for fathers.

"Flagstaff is only three hours from here. She could come visit every day if she really wanted to," I say with a laugh, and move away from Dad. He reaches for his glass of water and gulps it down.

"You haven't exactly made it easy for her," he says point blank, and I'm a little taken aback by his statement. "You always make it sound like it's an inconvenience for her to stay with you."

Do I make it harder than it should be? I always offer my bed to my parents, and I take the couch. I think back over the last year and realize this is the first time Mom and Dad have stayed over in almost two years. I always tell them I'm working or I'm busy. But it's true. I work all of the time. Except lately. Lately I've been working less and less at Eggceptional so I can spend time with Jordan. As the words tumble around in my head, it occurs to me that not only am I not spending time with my parents, but I've been spending way too much time away from Micah.

For so long there's never been any reason for me not to be with him—unless I was working. There's never been a man to take time away from my little boy, but now there's Jordan, distracting me. And it's a good distraction, one I've needed—one I've craved. I know I love him; I've loved him for eleven years, but is that enough?

"Are you ready to leave, Daniel?" Mom asks from outside the kitchen. Her eyes are puffy, giving away the real reason she rushed away. Behind her are their two suitcases, and Mom's purse is hanging off her shoulder.

I step toward her but she flinches, so I stop. "Mom, please don't leave like this. I don't want you to be upset."

"I'm fine, Regina. Ready, Daniel?"

"Abigail," Dad warns, and again Mom flinches.

"You need to apologize to your daughter for disrespecting her in her home."

"But—" Mom starts, but Dad cuts her off. I've never seen my dad speak to her like this; she's the one always calling the shots. As a matter of fact, I don't know that I've ever heard my dad *talk* this much.

"Apologize, hug, and then we can be on our way." Dad folds his arm across his broad chest and juts his chin out. Go, Dad!

Mom takes a hesitant step forward, and I decide to meet her in the middle. A hug is not something Mom wants, but if we're going to move past this block between us, a hug is what she's going to get. She chances a glance at me, clasps her hands in front of her waist, and then her shoulders sag in defeat. Her eyes well up again as her chin trembles.

"I'm sorry, Reggie," she says quietly. My heart bursts in my chest—she never calls me Reggie. "I just miss you and want you to be happy."

"I know, Mom," I say, pulling her in for a hug. She's ramrod straight, but I continue to hold on until she begins to soften, and finally—*finally!*—her arms wrap around me. We both burst into tears, gushing over each other until Dad clears his throat, clearly ready to leave. We say our goodbyes and, even though I wasn't sure how today was going to end, everything feels like it's going to be okay.

Chapter 29

Jordan

I've had a lot of time to pick apart the conversation between Reggie and whomever she was on the phone with up in Sedona. Something about it is nagging me, like a thorn buried in the fleshy part of my palm. It's annoying and hurts a little, but I'm choosing to trust her. My heart and soul are fragile, and I need to come out of this on top instead of stuck to the bottom of Reggie's shoe like discarded gum.

Tonight we're going out for a date, and I'm picking her up at her place. To some, it might not be a significant thing, but for me it means I've finally broken through whatever barrier she kept in place to keep me from her apartment. It's been a long four days and nights since we last kissed and I had to send her on her way. I should've taken her upstairs to the condo and showed her how much I love her. But a cold shower and a series of text messages over the next few days was what I got instead.

I pull into her complex and am sorely disappointed when she's waiting for me in the parking lot. What the hell? She's wearing a black and red patterned skirt that meets her ankles and a skinny tank top, revealing her bronzed shoulders. Her hair is pulled up into a messy knot on top of her head, making my fingers twitch to pull it out, letting her hair spill down her back.

Parking the car beside her, I climb out, step around the front, and say, "You ever heard of letting your man hold doors open for you and walk with you like a gentleman?" My tone is playful, but inside I'm a little irritated she didn't let me come up to her unit.

"You want to be a gentleman now?" she teases as she leans forward and presses her bright red lips to my cheek. She smells amazing, spicy with a hint of vanilla, and my earlier irritations are quickly fading.

I open the car door, place my hand on the small of her back, and help her into the seat. I lean down, guide the seatbelt across her lap, and touch my lips to hers in a gentle caress as the buckle clicks into place. She smiles, cheeks flushing a beautiful rose color I wish would stay on her face forever.

I've had a lot of time to evaluate the feelings I developed for Jemma almost two years ago, and though true love wasn't one of them, I believe she paved the way for me to make room in my heart for Reggie. Without Jemma's influence, I wouldn't be sitting here with my girl, driving our way through town to a cozy little European café in Gilbert. It's a bit of a drive, but the food is worth every mile.

"That's the fourth time you've yawned since you sat down," I say while I lace my fingers through hers across the center console. "You sure you're up for dinner tonight?"

Her lids lower before she glances back to me, smiling. "I'm good, just tired. It's been a busy four days and some very late nights. I really hope someday I don't have to work two jobs anymore. It's kicking my ass."

A laugh bubbles from my chest. If I have my way, that someday will be sooner than she realizes. I'm not talking marriage or a proposal, but there's no reason she should have to work two jobs when I have the means to help her financially. Then again, I'm curious why she works so hard, especially since she and Stacey share the apartment and theoretically she should only be responsible for half the rent.

Jokingly I ask, "Why do you work so much? Do you have an expensive habit I should be aware of?" Apparently that's the exact wrong thing to say to her, because her eyes widen and she purses her lips tightly. Shit. "I mean, do you? I kind of need to know before we go much farther. If it's drugs, then we can get through this, but you need to tell me."

She blinks. At least a dozen times. And I don't breathe, not even once.

Reggie clears her throat, and mine tightens, almost suffocating me. "You think I spend my money on drugs?"

And I exhale. A long, refreshing sigh of relief.

I shake my head and reach for her hand again. "No, Bug. It was supposed to be a joke, but your reaction scared me. I couldn't stop my mouth from running away with the thoughts floating through my head."

"Drugs?" She turns in her seat, her eyes drilling into mine. Thankfully we're stopped at a red light, because I'm squirming in my seat under her scrutiny. Her eyes narrow, and she folds her arms across her chest. "You of all people think I'm on drugs. That's…" Her cheeks puff out as she releases a breath. "I don't know what to say."

Apparently that sign should be back in place, you know, the one warning everyone what an asshole I can be. The light turns green, but instead of proceeding towards the restaurant, I turn right into a grocery store parking lot. There's no way I'm going to dinner with Reggie upset. I shift into park, remove my seatbelt, and open the door.

"Jordan, what are you doing?" Reggie asks before I exit the car, her voice clipped. My hands ball into fists and then release as I open her door. "Just get back in the car, Jordan," she says as she rolls her eyes.

I kneel down in the black asphalt, brace my hands on the doorframe, and stare into her eyes, memorizing the gold flecks interspersed with the dark chocolate brown.

"I do not now, or ever, believe you're using, Reggie. I'm an insecure asshole who was stupidly curious why you work two jobs when you have a roommate. I know you're better than drugs, better than me, and I hope you'll forgive me for making you feel less than you are." My hand moves on its own to her cheek, and her eyes flutter closed as she inhales sharply. "I'm sorry, Reggie-bug. Please forgive me."

She sighs and nods, making my heart feel as though it's been jump-started. She leans into my palm and then moves forward but is jerked back in her seat. Her eyes widen and then a high-pitched laugh tumbles from her mouth. I drop my hand and stand up, feeling more confused than ever.

Reggie unclicks the seatbelt and leaps to her feet in front of me. "I'm sorry." She giggles. "The seatbelt locked up." Her grin goes from playful to demure as she tucks her chin to her chest. Groaning, I pull her into me and wrap my arms around her. She fits there, as though she was made just for me. It feels warm and safe and good. Damn good.

"You're not better than me," she whispers as she glances up at me, lashes fluttering against her olive skin. "And of course I forgive you. I'm sorry I overreacted. I'm just so tired and on edge."

I hold her tighter, press my lips to her forehead, and inhale her spicy vanilla scent. I realize it's something that reminds me of comfort, of being home in the arms of the one you love.

"Anything I can do to help take the edge off?"

Reggie's shoulders begin to shake as she giggles against my chest. "Kiss me," she says as her hands climb over my chest, stopping at the back of my neck. Her tongue darts out and slowly licks her red lips, and it's like I'm a mirror, reflecting her actions—my tongue copies hers. She stands on the tips of her toes, and I lower my head to meet her open, waiting lips. It's not a kiss filled with heat or passion, but long and slow that builds and builds until I'm no longer hungry for dinner. We break away, breathless, and I force myself to move three steps back. Reggie's cheeks are flushed and, as she returns to the car, I turn to adjust myself before walking to the driver's side.

Dinner is delicious—it always is here. Thankfully I know the owner and have the privilege of ordering off his secret menu. When Reggie's had her fill of the pasta I ordered for her, she pushes the plate away, leans back in her chair, and rubs her tummy.

"Thank goodness I wore this skirt," she says with a laugh. "It hides my food baby."

I glance at her, cocking my brow in question. "Food baby?"

"You know when you eat so much it looks like you're pregnant."

I laugh and enjoy how her cheeks flush again. And then as strange as it may seem, I try to imagine what Reggie would look like while pregnant. Would her belly be round like a basketball or stick out like a torpedo? Would she waddle or get swollen feet? I scan her body, stopping at her "food baby," and am hit with the cold realization that I would love to make a baby with her someday. But I'd probably make a horrible father since mine wasn't exactly the best example to me. I shake off the thought, knowing I've got a lot of growing up and staying clean before that dream ever comes to fruition.

"You ready to head out?" I ask after I pay the bill and scoop the mints off the leather check folder and hand them to Reggie. She quickly snatches them from my hand, smiling wide, and drops them into her tiny purse. She nods, and we make our way back to my car.

Neither one of us is ready to call it a night even though Reggie has to work both jobs tomorrow. We drive up the road to the theater and catch a movie that just started, even though neither of us knows anything about it. We sit in the front row so we can put our feet up on the bars in front of us and settle in for the next ninety minutes. Halfway through the car chases and flying bullets, Reggie falls asleep against my shoulder. I kiss the top of her head, move in the chair to stand up, and then gently stroke her cheek. She stirs beneath my touch, slowly opens her eyes, and smiles.

"Let's get you home, Bug," I say, helping her to her feet and tucking her into my side as we walk to my car where I get her buckled and ready to go. Her hands cup my cheeks as she pulls my lips to hers.

"I love you, Jordan Capshaw," she says, smiling against my mouth. "I hope you know that." I move to stand upright, but she grips my shoulders, speaks drowsily with her eyes nearly closed. "I'm sorry I'm so tired. I wish we could go back to your place for some alone time. I don't have any privacy at my place. I never know when Micah will show up."

Her hands drop to the seat, taking my heart right along with them. Who the hell is Micah? And what is he doing showing up at my girl's apartment?

I close her door and sit on the hood of my car, trying to piece together a scenario where my life makes sense. One minute I don't know if I can love this woman any more than I already do, and then the next minute it feels like someone's fist is wrapped around my heart and they're trying as hard

199

as they can to pull it out from between my ribs. I'm an idiot to think she wouldn't have some other guy showing up to take her from me. She probably has dozens of guys knocking on her door. The woman is perfection defined, in looks and personality. When does that ever really happen?

Back inside the car, I drive across town, stewing in the silence. Reggie's soft snores are the only things keeping me company, and honestly, at this moment, I'm not sure I even want those.

"We're here, Reggie," I say, hovering over her. I purposely parked illegally against the curb, knowing I have no intention of following her inside. Her exhaustion is obviously the only reason for the slip. She'd probably never have told me otherwise, and the thought makes me want to push her out of the car.

Reggie wakes with a yawn, her arms rising over her head in an exaggerated stretch. She smiles as I help her out of the car.

"I'm sorry I was so tired," she says, yawning once more. "I'll stay awake next time, okay?"

I can only manage a tight-lipped smile and an awkward hug, but apparently it's good enough for her since she gives me a quick kiss on my cheek and runs up the stairs to her apartment.

I have suddenly developed an all-out, raging hate for all guys named Micah.

Chapter 30

Reggie

Micah's birthday party is next Saturday. I still can't believe my little man will be eight—where has the time gone? The day I found out I was pregnant with him was one of the worst days of my life. The breakup with Jordan was still so fresh, my heart was broken and even though it was me who ended the relationship, I still cried into my pillow every night. To the world I appeared fine, that the breakup didn't matter. But the truth was I loved him too much not to let him go, knowing he was going to make something of himself, and I didn't want to be the one to hold him back.

When the nausea showed up, followed by the extreme fatigue, I knew something wasn't right. Stacey marched me to the drug store where she bought me a pregnancy test. The pink box in my hand felt like a bomb about to explode. I didn't want to hold it and have it confirm my suspicions.

Stacey sat with me in the bathroom of Walgreens

while I peed on the stick. It didn't even take the allotted three minutes to show up positive. I cried even more after that, realizing my life was about to seriously change. The morning sickness hit me at all times of the day, making it impossible to hide the pregnancy from my parents. After they learned the truth, Mom yelled at me and told me I needed to move out, saying if I was old enough to have sex and get pregnant, then I was old enough to be on my own. Thank goodness for Stacey, because she went out with me that day and, with the help of her parents, signed a lease for an apartment. We moved in that night and have been living together ever since.

Now, I have this wonderful boy browsing the aisles of Whole Foods with me, searching for a specific gluten-free cupcake mix I need for only one boy at the party. Everyone else can eat the crap I apparently feed my son. Back when I was younger there was no such thing as gluten-free anything, and kids got along eating the same stuff as everyone else. Now it's like we have to cater to each allergy or food-related issue known to man. I mean, come on, it's a birthday party for eight-year-olds.

"Finally," I say with a sigh, pulling the mix off the shelf. Micah beams up at me as he picks out the cake mix he wants for his real cupcakes and hands me the box. Devil's Food Cake—he is totally my son. I grab a tub of dark chocolate frosting and another of gluten-free vanilla and check my list for anything else I can grab here.

"Can I have ice cream for my party too, Mom?" Micah asks, batting his eyelashes. I hang the basket over the crook of my elbow, muss his hair, and pull him toward me.

"Of course," I say, giving him a quick squeeze. "What my boy wants for his party, he gets." Micah's eyes widen in disbelief as his lips open in a massive smile. He's so happy he does a series of five quick jumps and pumps his fist in the air.

"I want the one with chocolate, vanilla, and strawberry," he says eagerly. My son is the only kid I know who actually likes Neapolitan ice cream. He loves to let it soften and then swirl the three flavors together so it creates a gooey gray mess he can dip his cake into.

"You do realize you're the only one who likes that kind, right?"

His smile widens as he shakes his head and runs toward the freezer section in the back of the store. I pass the bread aisle, grab a yummy-looking whole wheat bread with an assortment of nuts on the crust, and toss it in the basket. As I get closer to the ice cream, where Micah is trying to reach the kind he wants from the top of the freezer, my feet literally stop walking. It's like they've suddenly been cemented in place.

The sight I'm viewing from twenty feet away makes my heart feel like bursting from my chest and running forward to usher my boy back to me. Heat and shame cover my body as though I've suddenly developed a fever, and I break out into a light sweat.

And then Micah is handed a small carton of Neapolitan ice cream, and his cheeks puff out in a smile that breaks my heart. He then turns, points to me, and everything that has taken place over the past month flashes through my mind like a black-and-white movie.

Jordan is walking this way, his hand on my son's—*his* son's—shoulder, wearing a look of sheer confusion. His eyes are narrowed, his lips are pulled into a tight line, and his shoulders are stiff. Seven paces between us, and he glances to Micah and then back at me and then back to Micah.

Three paces.

Oh shit.

"Reggie?" he says sharply, though there is also a questioning tone to his voice.

I swallow, because I can't do anything else. I feel like I'm sinking, like I'm taking a bath in quicksand and it's pulling me through the dark tile of the grocery store. Jordan's face is a mask of confusion that quickly turns to anger and all I can do is sink further and further into the pit of lies I've created.

"Is he your son?" Jordan asks, once again glancing between me and Micah. Micah steps away from Jordan, his face twisted with worry. He grabs my hand and pulls me to his level.

"Mom? Are you okay?" he asks as I pull him close. Jordan takes two steps back, and that muscle tick in his jaw is back while he stares at my arms around Micah.

"Dammit, Reggie. You should have told me you had a kid," he says before turning around and walking away. The words I want to say are stuck in my throat, lodged somewhere between my shock and the apology he's owed. I want to run after him and confess everything, tell him about our son and how wonderful he is. Show him this little boy who's growing into a young man and how they share the same eye color and nose. But I've lost my chance. He's walked away, and I'm clinging to my son, tears streaming down my face in the middle of the bread aisle.

People step around us, avoiding eye contact and whispering, but never once do they stop to ask if we're okay. What would I tell them? That I've just screwed up the one chance I had at love? I want to laugh, scream, pull out my hair. I was given a second chance with the man I've been in love with for years and I kept him away from the only other good thing in my life. What's worse is what he's going to do when he finds out Micah is his son.

Fresh tears spill down my face, and it's all I can do to sit against the grocery shelving and not curl into a ball on the floor.

"Mommy, the ice cream's melting," Micah says as he twists his lips like he does when he's nervous. My poor son is squatting next to me, running his hand over my hair, looking at me like he's not sure if I'm all right. I'm not okay, but I need to be strong for him now.

"I'm sorry, honey," I say, swiping away the tears with my index fingers. "Mommy's going to be okay. Let's go home." There's no use trying to hide the mess I am, so I stand up, grab the basket, and walk with Micah to the checkout counter. The middle-aged woman at the register glances at me, and her eyes nearly bug out.

"Such sad faces on you two," she says with a pleasant smile. "Chin up; tomorrow is another day."

She winks at Micah, scans our food, and bags it all up. As she hands me our groceries, she pats my shoulder and says, "Nothing is worth crying that hard over, dear. You go on home, take a long soak in the bath, and put on a smile for that little boy of yours. A hot bath can solve just about anything."

She sends us on our way with another wink. Ha! I wish a long, hot bath would cure me of my guilt and bring Jordan back to me. If only I could go back to all those years ago when I found out I was pregnant. Maybe it was selfish of me to keep it a secret. I truly believed by not telling Jordan about Micah that he could go on to live the life he always wanted and I'd never see him again. I never imagined a scenario where Jordan and I were dating again.

Somehow I manage to make it through the rest of the day without breaking down in front of Micah. Stacey arrives home about an hour after I put Micah to bed, and that's when the floodgates open. I nearly hyperventilate reliving the encounter with Jordan. While I cry like a baby, she hugs me on the couch and hands me tissue after tissue.

"If I'd have known what I was coming home to, I would have come prepared with Tonight Dough ice cream," she says, making us both laugh. Stacey brushes her hand through my hair, hands me another tissue, and leans back against the couch.

"Have you heard from him yet?" she asks as I sniff back the last of my tears.

I shake my head in an attempt to clear the crazy thoughts running through my head, but all it does is make the hurt more real. I've really, truly lost him this time.

"He'll call when he's had some time to calm down. When it finally hits him that he has a son, he'll call."

Tears. Another sob slips out as I pull more tissues from the box and blow my nose. "I didn't tell him that Micah is his. There wasn't enough time before he walked away."

Stacey closes her eyes and sighs. "Reggie," she says as a warning. When she opens her eyes she stares right at me, making me feel about an inch tall.

"I know, Stacey. But how can I tell him now? What if he never wants to talk to me again?"

"Send him a text to see if you guys can talk. Let him take the lead. Heaven knows he's going to have another hard choice once you tell him the whole truth."

I nod, grab my phone, and type out a dozen texts before settling on one.

Me: *I'm sorry I didn't tell you about my son. Can we please talk?*

And now I wait.
And wait.

Chapter 31

Jordan

She has a kid. My girl has a kid, and she never thought of mentioning him to me. I want to punch my fist through a wall, not because I'm angry, but because I gave Reggie my heart and it feels like she tore it from under my ribs and used it for a damn trampoline. A kid. This hurts on a whole new level.

I couldn't buy the groceries in my cart. I just left them sitting next to the freezer section and walked out of the store. Now I sit here in my car, hands gripping the steering wheel like it's the only thing keeping me grounded. Like any moment I could float away to a world where the woman I love never lied to me about having a kid.

She has a kid.

What the hell am I supposed to do with this information? I never signed up to fall into the role of a father, and that's exactly what I'd be doing if we continue down this path. Shit. I release the steering wheel only to slam my hands back down on it. The kid has a dad out there somewhere, which means in some sick way, I'd have to share Reggie with him. No way is that ever happening.

I turn the key and peel out of the parking lot before I have to see Reggie and her kid walk out of the building. I can't be here to see that—I'm not ready. But I'm ready for a drink, and I don't care if that means throwing away the last twenty-one months of sobriety. This kind of news isn't for the weak.

And right now I'm about as weak as a sapling in winter.

The street names don't register while I drive through Phoenix. The buildings pass by in a blur, and it's only when I nearly run a red light that I snap out of it enough to pay attention to my driving. Today is not a good day to die.

But it's a great day to drink.

Any bar will do at this point; I just need to find one. How, after fifteen minutes of driving, have I not found a place to get a drink? And then, as if by magic, one appears. It's a hole-in-the-wall near the base of the mountain. The bar appears inviting with its sapphire blue door amidst the desert-gold stucco. The parking lot is nothing but tiny bits of gravel, and there's a hitching rail on the side of the building. Huh. Drinking and horseback riding, who knew?

I climb out of the car, pull on the rubberized door handle—in the summer the metal can give you third-degree burns—and step inside the dimly lit bar. It smells like cigarettes and beer, making my mouth water with need. The Saltillo tiled floors look as though it's been ages since they've seen the wet side of a mop, and the crowd is small. As long as they serve alcohol, I'm drinking.

The bar is long, with enough seating for about twenty people, and the shelves on the back wall are well stocked. It's only a little before lunch, which means I've got the rest of the day and most of the night to put a good dent in those bottles.

"Whatcha drinking?" the man behind the counter asks. He's about my age, though completely bald and tatted all over his arms and neck. The guy could probably bench-press a small car with those arms that are as round as my thighs.

I survey the liquor behind the bar and settle on my old favorite. "Give me a bottle of Wild Turkey and a shot glass."

"Can't give you the bottle, man, but I can pour the shots all night long. Name's Colt when you need another." Colt turns, pulls an opened bottle of the whiskey from the shelf, slides an empty shot glass my way, and then fills it nearly to the brim with the amber liquid. My trembling fingers grip the small glass, and the scent of sweet corn and vanilla hits me as he pours. My heart pounds feverishly in my chest, and the Wild Turkey ripples in the shot glass due to my shaking hand.

Get a grip, Jordan. It's just a drink; it's not going to kill you. Something in my stomach lurches as I scoot the glass closer, and I just can't find it within myself to lift the shot off the bar. It's like the alcohol is dead weight and no matter how much I try to lift it off the counter, I can't. Maybe I need something else?

"Colt," I call down the bar. He glances up from his phone and struts over, puffing out his black t-shirt covered chest.

"'Sup?" he asks with a flick of his head. "Something wrong with the whiskey?"

"No, man. I'm just not feeling this one. Give me something stronger maybe?"

Colt nods while reaching for the Wild Turkey, but I stop him by grabbing his forearm. His eyes narrow, and his nostrils flare—don't touch the bartender, got it.

"Sorry," I say. "I'll keep it in case I change my mind."

A moment later, Colt returns with a lowball glass, a couple ice cubes resting at the bottom. He pours some Jim Beam Black over the ice and then steps away. Now I have two drinks, one for each hand, and I still can't drink them. What is wrong with me?

Ha! That's a loaded question. It's more like what *isn't* wrong with me? Why, when shit goes bad like it did today, do I crave a drink? Why am I sitting here with two drinks in my hand and unable to actually gulp them down? Even though I want to— so damn bad. Why in the hell was I made to crave substances that can kill me and hurt those I love? I just want to slam down these drinks, but then what does that say about me? I'm a piece of shit loser who can't keep his head straight. That's what it says. Just like my father used to tell me over and over. Despite Roger thinking it would be a good idea to patch things up with my parents, the words my dad said are something I can't ever un-hear, and no matter how much someone might beg for forgiveness, those words are still there. They hang around like a scar or a tattoo and never leave despite trying to cover them up. I will always be the disappointment my father made me believe I was. Always.

"You okay, man?" Colt asks, appearing in front of me after a while. "You've been here almost an hour and still haven't taken a drink." He glances down at the two glasses then back at me, his brow creased. "Want me to call someone for you?"

"No," I answer enthusiastically, which causes a few heads to turn my way. Waving them off, I grab the glass of Jim Beam and pick it up and pull it to my lips. The spicy scent and burn of alcohol hits my nose, making me gag. I slam the glass on the counter and motion to Colt that I'll be back. I've got to get my shit together.

Quickly finding the bathroom in the back of the bar, I step inside and lock the door, thankful for a single toilet. The faucet is older, the kind where you have to actually twist the knobs, so I turn the cold on full blast. I let it run while I lean over the sink with my hands on the ledge. I still don't like to look in the mirror, and today is no exception.

When I walked inside the bar, I expected the feel of the glass to be like a friend I haven't seen in years. I thought it would be easy—*natural*—to down a shot of whiskey. But everything in this bar is mocking me, telling me what a failure I am. How I can't manage to deal with my issues like a normal, *rational* person.

The sink is filling up despite the missing drain

plug, so I quickly turn off the water before sinking my hands in the chilly water. For a moment it almost stings, but the slight pain is welcome as it dulls a small part of me. I splash water over my face, thrilled with the way it feels like the sting of a slap. This is exactly what I need, an icy pool to dive into, to dull the ache in my chest.

A hard knock on the door interrupts my solitude, earning a string of muttered curses directed at the guy outside. I pull a few paper towels from the dispenser to dry my hands, toss them in the trash, and then open the door to an old man so wrinkled I can't imagine he ever looked young.

"About time," Wrinkles says through a toothless, shriveled mouth. He brushes past me and slams the door.

Colt hasn't taken my drinks away. He jerks his head in greeting as I sit down and resume my position of holding both drinks in my hands. Both drinks are whiskey, both will dull the ache in my chest, yet in my hands they taunt me, filling me with guilt.

I dip my index finger into the Jim Beam, noting the ice has already melted, pull it out, and bring it to my lips. If I just let this single drop forming on the tip of my finger fall into my mouth, maybe that will get me over this hump. As the drop grows and threatens to drop, Colt is suddenly in front of me and uses a bar rag to dry my finger. I pull my hand away quickly and slam it down on the bar.

"What the hell, man?" My voice is strained from trying not to shout at him for ruining the chance I was giving myself to get over this…fear.

"Don't do it," he says as he crosses his massive arms over his burly chest. "I've been where you are, and if it weren't for some asshole stopping me, I wouldn't be here today."

"Yeah, well, this is a shitty place to work for an alcoholic," I deadpan, then shove the glasses toward him.

"This is my bar, asswipe."

"Like I said, pretty shitty place to work for an alcoholic."

"This place saved my life." Colt snatches my drinks from the edge of the bar and dumps the alcohol into the sink. He pulls a highball from the back counter, fills it with water and ice, and hands it to me. "This one's on the house," he says with a laugh. "Those other two will cost you a Benjamin."

I choke on the water and slam the glass on the bar a little too hard, though it thankfully doesn't shatter

"A hundred bucks? Hell no," I say, shoving the water back toward him.

"I figure your plan was to down at least two bottles, so you might as well feel the sting in your wallet for your poor intentions."

"Poor intentions or not, you wouldn't charge Wrinkles over there fifty bucks for two bottles of whiskey, would you?" I point to the old man, who notices and gives me the bird.

"Old Roy?" Colt laughs, bringing his hands to the edge of the bar. "Yeah, I'd make him give me his granddaughter for that. She is one fine-looking woman." Um, okay? I glance to Old Roy and wonder what kind of spawn he could make that

214

would produce a good-looking woman.

"Whatever does it for you, man." I pull my wallet from my front pocket and pull out the cash for the drinks I didn't consume, and prepare to leave, but Colt pins me in the seat with a glare.

"Working here, owning this bar, it's not easy, and sometimes, yes, it's a shitty place to work. But it's mine. I own it, and I wouldn't trade working here for a single drop of liquor, ever." Colt wipes down the bar in front of me with his bar rag and then steps back, leaning against the narrow counter behind him. "So if I can own a bar and work in it seven days a week, then you, Jordan Capshaw, can leave here without taking a drink too."

I figured he knew who I was, so he's fully aware of my current sobriety status—the entire world is.

"Why did you pour me a drink if you knew all about me? You ever think you may be in the wrong line of work if you're serving alcoholics and drug addicts booze?"

Colt erupts into deep laughter and crosses his massive arms over his chest. "You know what, Jordan? I like you; you're good people. How did you find yourself in the middle of old Phoenix in my bar?"

And just like that I spill the contents of my day to him like we've been best friends since birth. They say women tell all their secrets to their hairdressers; if that's true, then men share with their bartenders. Colt listens while I explain to him how I won't share Reggie with another man or that I don't have a great example of a father figure to model myself after. When I finish dumping my worries on

215

him, he stands back, arms crossed over his chest, and appraises me for longer than I feel is necessary.

Finally, he speaks. "So what you're saying is you're chicken shit." His arms drop as he steps toward me and places his hands on the counter, leaning in.

"Anyone ever tell you that you're a scary S.O.B.?" I ask, leaning back a bit to escape his pinning glare.

"Face it, Jordan. You totally freaked out and abandoned the woman you love in the middle of a freaking grocery store to deal with her feelings. Shit, man. You royally screwed the pooch."

"Yeah, I can see that now. What would you have done?" I'd like to see what he thinks would've been a better way to play out the scenario. When he bends over, resting his elbows on the bar, his shoulders drop a bit. Thank God, because he was scary intimidating leaning over me like that.

"Sure, I probably would have been a little mad, shocked for sure. But I'm pretty sure I wouldn't have left her alone to deal with everything on her own. You didn't even give her a chance to explain anything."

I bury my face in my hands and hope I can get my shit together enough to talk to her, figure out where to go from here. It's time to find out if I have what it takes to be a father figure or not. At this given moment, sitting in a bar, I'm the worst kind of person that neither Reggie nor her son need.

"Thanks, Colt," I say, slapping his hand and giving it a good shake. "You're a better bartender than I gave you credit for. See ya around."

Step one: get my shit together.
Step two: talk to my girl.

Chapter 32

Reggie

I'm late. No, not *that* kind of late—that all turned out fine. I'm talking the kind of late that is going to earn me a firm reprimand from my boss. I didn't want to go in to Eggceptional tonight after the day I had, but I didn't have a choice. I didn't want to go in looking like a blotchy-faced mess, so I showered, applied some concealer under my eyes, and showed up forty minutes late.

Rico greets me at the kitchen, his spatula in hand, and clucks his tongue at my tardiness.

"It's a good thing I like you so much and covered for you when the boss called," he teases as he points the greasy utensil in my direction. "What in the refried beans is wrong with you?" he asks as his eyes take in my puffy face. Hugs from Rico really are the best, because he doesn't offer anything but friendship. He pulls me in and fresh tears spring to my face, but I quickly dry them and step away.

"That man of yours giving you trouble?" he asks as he flips a series of pancakes.

I shake my head, swallow back tears, and clear my throat. "No, not exactly," I say, and then proceed to tell him how Jordan found out I have a son.

"And the jerk just took off, leaving you in the store?" I should probably mention that Rico is married and has seven kids at home—seven daughters—and he's well aware of the drama that follows us. "Did you tell him who Micah's father is?" Rico glances as me, a curious expression on his face. Other than my parents and Stacey, I haven't ever told anyone else who Micah's father is. Looking back now, maybe I should have, because the secrets have grown and grown, only to explode in my face.

"No, and I'm not sure he's going to give me a chance to tell him." I haven't heard from Jordan after I sent the text earlier, and it's killing me. For all I know, he could've been so upset that he took off and ran his car into a ditch and is dying on the side of the road.

Rico gives me another quick hug and sends me out on the floor to do my rounds. Somehow I make it through my late shift and arrive home without incident. Still no texts from Jordan, and I suspect I may not hear from him again.

***

Sunday passes in a blur, and Micah is off to school Monday morning. I'm back to work at the rental agency, still with no word from Jordan. I'm so tired from the lack of sleep. Anything and everything makes me cry, including some commercial on the radio this morning about a new weight-loss system that has changed people's lives.

I thought my life was going to change, that by some miracle Jordan and I would make things work and I'd have my happy little family. But I was stupid and hid the one thing that could tear us apart. It's time to stop wallowing; I can't go back and change anything now.

By the end of the workday, I give a mental thanks to the Universe that I don't have any shifts at Eggceptional tonight. Stacey and Micah have dinner ready when I arrive home, and it smells divine.

"Teriyaki chicken and rice, if you're hungry," Stacey says as she dishes up her and Micah's plates.

"Look, Mom," Micah practically squeals. "I helped Auntie make dinner."

I wrap my arms around my boy in a tight hug and tell him how proud I am. He's been showing a lot of interest in cooking lately, and I'm grateful Stacey is so patient and willing to indulge him in his creativity when I'm not here. All three of us sit down to eat, and I have to admit the food makes me feel a lot better, though I'm still so tired I could probably sleep for a week.

We spend the rest of the night playing board games in the living room until Micah can no longer keep his eyes open. Sometimes I rebel against standard parenting and let my boy stay up late on a school night. After the weekend I've had, a night like this was exactly what I needed. Micah yawns, closes his light brown eyes, and I declare the night over. He pads barefoot down the hall to his bedroom and, after Stacey and I have cleaned up the games, I go tuck him into bed.

The light is on in his room when I walk through the door, but he's passed out on top of his *Pokémon* comforter, still in the clothes he's been wearing all day. Pulling him up to his pillow, I pull his blankets up and give him a quick kiss on his forehead. As I stand at his doorway, I can't help but marvel at my boy, knowing he's the source of joy in my life and has been since the day he was born. Then it hits me; I already have the family I've always wanted. Even though we're not a traditional husband, wife, and kids family, Micah is enough. He will always be enough. Stacey too.

A hand on my shoulder startles me, and when I turn, Stacey is standing behind me, a worried look on her face.

"Can we talk?" she asks, making my newly found happy realization take a tumble down through my stomach. I follow her back to the living room where we both plop onto the couch and sigh. I'm guessing for different reasons.

"I know you've had a really crappy weekend," she says, pulling a pillow from behind her back and laying it on her lap. This is a signature move when she's nervous about something. Sadly, my defenses raise, and I begin sweating. Stacey hasn't been nervous around me for years.

"I'm pretty sure I'm only going to make it worse." She glances down at her fingers and picks at a hangnail. Oh God. No. No, no, no.

"Stacey." My voice floats from my mouth like the softest whisper. My eyes begin to sting, and the back of my throat twinges. Please don't say it. *Please*.

"I love you," she says in a rush. "You're the sister I never had, and living with you has been amazing."

I'm finding it difficult to breathe, and my heart is pounding in my ears, making her voice sound like it's coming from underwater.

"I don't know how to say this without hurting you, so I'm just going to come right out and say it." She pauses, takes a deep breath, and runs all her words together. "But it's time I move out and find who I am on my own." Now we're both crying, tears slipping down our faces and noses sniffling. Neither of us moves to console the other, and it feels like a deep chasm has been created suddenly and the gaping hole between us is black and deep.

"What am I going to do without you?" Somehow I manage to squeak out one of the many questions I have. "Are you mad at me?"

"No," she says quickly. "It's just time, Reggie. We both need to find out who we are and what we want out of life. Neither of us can do it while relying on the other person all the time."

"What am I going to tell Micah? You're like a second mother to him."

Stacey gasps and brings her hands to her face, shielding the tears slipping down her cheeks. "I love that boy like he's my own. That's part of the problem, Reggie. He's not my son, but there are days when I feel like he is. And I want that. I want kids of my own, but I'm never going to get that by living here with you." Her words are muffled from covering her face, but I receive the message loud and clear. She's moving on; she wants a life outside of me and Micah. I get it. I really do. But it still hurts, and it will be so strange not to have my best friend here with us.

Fresh tears pool along my bottom lids and then fall like heavy raindrops, landing on my pants in dark, wet circles. I need to gather my strength, support her as she's supported me throughout the years and be there for her every step of the way. If anyone deserves it, it's her.

I slide across the couch, toss her lap pillow on the floor, and pull her in for a hug, which only makes us both sob harder. Through our hiccup-riddled tears, we relive some of our best memories and laugh a little too.

"I'm going to miss you so much," I say, wiping my face and sniffing back the last of my tears. Stacey dabs her face with a tissue and echoes my sniffing. Together we must look like quite the pair.

"I'm going to miss you and Micah so much. I'm not sure I know how to adult on my own, you know? I still feel eighteen sometimes, but it's time to grow up and take life a little more seriously now."

"When will you move out?" Stacey hands me a couple tissues, and I wipe under my eyes, revealing a big, black mascara mess. Awesome.

"My place will be ready in three weeks," she says with another sniffle. *Three weeks?*

"So soon." My stomach sinks to my knees.

"Where will you be living? Please tell me you're not moving in with the MMA guy."

Stacey cringes, scrunching up her freckled nose. She shakes her head enthusiastically. "Hell no," she says with gusto. "That ended shortly after the Vegas trip."

"What happened? He didn't hurt you, did he?"

"Hardly. Let's just say his muscles and physique weren't exactly natural, and the 'roids have seriously affected his—"

"Whoa, okay. TMI," I say with a giggle. We both have a good laugh, but a chime sounds nearby, indicating an incoming text message. The breath catches in my throat as I leap off the couch to grab my phone from the kitchen counter.

It's Jordan. Breathe in. Breathe out.

Jordan: I'm sorry I walked away. Can we meet up tomorrow?

"Jordan wants to get together tomorrow," I say, returning to the couch to sit next to Stacey. She pulls my hair off my neck and pats my shoulder. "What should I tell him?"

"You owe him an explanation, Reggie. And you should do it here so he can meet his son." She's right. His reaction in the grocery store won't hold a candle to the one he'll have here. My stomach twists into knots when I send off a reply.

Me: Meet me at my place, 6 p.m.? I want you to meet Micah. I'll cook dinner.

One breath passes. Two.

Jordan: K.

Nervous doesn't begin to describe how I'm feeling. How sick. Like, quite literally, I could throw up right now from how my stomach is pitching and rolling. I'm never going to be able to sleep tonight, and I have no idea how I'm going to make it through work tomorrow.

Chapter 33

Jordan

Jeremy hasn't been home all weekend, and desperate times call for desperate measures. I text him an S.O.S. message and within twenty minutes he's barreling through the front door of the condo like a crazed maniac. He braces his hands on the doorframe, his hair is a disaster, and his eyes scan the entire condo. Not quite the normal picture of Jeremy. He's going to kill me for interrupting his night with Emily.

"Dude, where is it? Give it to me," he says, almost breathlessly. Finally walking through the door, I can see he is actually out of breath.

"What did you do, man, run all the way from Emily's place?"

He leans over the back of the couch, his arms resting on the back aiding in his stooped position.

"The elevator was taking too long, so I ran up the stairs." A sweat droplet drips down the side of his face, and I burst into laughter. "The hell? You texted an S.O.S., Jordan. I got here as fast as I could."

He's still glancing around the room, expecting to find my stash of drugs or alcohol at the very least. But he's not going to find it. After I left Colt's bar, I called Roger and we met up at a steakhouse and talked about why I almost gave in to the temptation of drinking. Not only did talking with him confirm my decision to abstain from alcohol, but also my suspicions about going anywhere near a bar being a pretty bad idea.

"I didn't S.O.S. you because I was thinking about using, JD. I texted you because I need to talk to you about Reggie."

Jeremy's features visibly relax. He walks around the couch and sits against the opposite arm from me. He props one leg up on the coffee table, raises his brows in question, and lounges like he owns the place.

"If this is because you knocked her up, I'm gonna be pissed," he says with a chuckle. He shakes his head then leans it against the back cushions.

I lace my fingers behind my neck, blow out a deep breath, and ready myself to unleash the weekend on him. "No, she's not pregnant. At least, she hasn't been in a while."

Jeremy's eyes bug out as he says, "Okay?"

"She has a kid, man. A boy. He's probably six or seven years old."

"Who's the father? Is he in the picture?" Jeremy asks, now sitting fully upright.

I shrug my shoulders, then rest my chin on my hand. "I have no idea. I'm going to go talk to her later tonight at her place." I realize I'm being a jerk not asking about how him and Emily are getting along, so I clear my throat and ask, "How's, uh, Emily doing? Still pregnant?"

A smile filled with pride takes over Jeremy's face, and I feel a pang of jealousy. Not that I particularly want a kid, but why does Reggie have to have one with someone other than me?

"Yeah, man. She's doing great. We actually went to her doctor last week and got to hear the heartbeat."

"So you're okay with the whole thing? What are you going to do when the baby comes?" What I'm really asking is what's going to happen to White Shadow?

"I'm out, Jordan. We have our last recording session in a couple weeks and after that, I'm done. I've had a good run, but I'm happy with Emily. We're good together." He laughs, slapping a hand on his knee. "Actually, better than good. We're great. I know it's quick, but I love her. We're going to drive up to Vegas in April and get hitched."

Whoa. This is extremely unexpected news to me.

"Wow. That's really great. I'm happy for you." Thinking about it, what I've just said, I am happy for him. JD is one of the best people I know, and I want nothing but happiness for him. He deserves it.

"What's your plan with Reggie? The kid?" he asks as he leans back against the couch again.

"Honestly, I haven't got a clue. I guess I'll hear her out tonight and sleep on it. I'm not exactly the dad type, but I might try. I love Reggie; think I always have."

"Dude, you're the only one who didn't know it. We all did, and when you two broke up it really messed with you. And then all the partying took its toll." Jeremy sighs then shakes his head, clearing the memories. "Anyway, that's over and in the past, and you two are back together. If you really love her, you'll figure it out."

*   *   *

I'm a nervous wreck. After talking with Jeremy I felt good. Really good. But here I sit in my car outside Reggie's apartment with sweaty palms and a heart beating wildly out of control. I need to pull myself together before I head up those stairs and back into her life. *His* life. Jesus. How am I going to do this?

A text chimes on my phone, making me even more jumpy.

Jeremy: *Good luck, bro.*

I'm so nervous I can't respond to his text, so instead I shove my phone into the center console and step out into the cool evening air. It's now or never. My feet drag like I'm walking through chilled molasses as I cross the parking lot. Each step to Reggie's door is torture as gravity attempts to pull me back down. By the time I raise my hand to knock on her door, my chest is tight and I'm practically panting from the effort it took to get here.

The kid—Micah—he's six or seven, maybe

older. I recall the way his eyes radiated pleasure when I handed him the Neapolitan ice cream at Whole Foods and how they caught me off guard. Brown eyes are common; they come in a variety of shades.

I knock. Three times.

There was fear written all over Reggie's face when she hugged her son. The way her eyes immediately glossed over with unshed tears. *Shit*.

The door swings open, and I'm greeted by a pair of big, light brown eyes and a mop of dark brown hair. He blinks, opens the door all the way, and then disappears down a hallway. I knock again, step inside, and close the door.

"Reggie?" I call, turning toward a rustling sound on my left.

"In here," she answers. I find her in the kitchen, pulling a pan out of the oven. She's wearing a pair of dark blue skinny jeans and a slouchy black top that accentuates the curves she has underneath. Her hair is tied back in a low ponytail that I wish I could twirl around my fingers. "Hey," she says casually. Her lips quirk into an uneasy smile, though it fades quickly.

"Can I help you?" I ask, noticing the small table is set for three. She shakes her head, places the pan in the center of her table, and finally looks at me. Her kitchen is small, just two rows of light oak cabinets with a fridge, sink, dishwasher, and stove that lead to an eat-in nook.

"Dinner's ready, if you want to sit down. I'll go get Micah." She ducks around me, leaving me alone in the kitchen and wondering where she wants me to sit. I don't want to screw anything up, so I decide to stand in front of the sink until she comes back.

Reggie and Micah round the corner, and the air literally catches in my chest. She scoots her son in front, places her hands lovingly on his shoulders, and gazes up at me.

"Jordan, this is Micah." She pauses, swallows slowly, and takes a deep breath.

Do I say hi? Shake his hand? Shit, I have no freaking clue what to do. My heart feels like a caged animal desperate to escape; it's roaring and tearing at the walls keeping it locked inside. Before I have time to react, Micah tugs on the hem of Reggie's black shirt. She kneels down wearing a hesitant smile. He leans in close and whispers loud enough for me to hear. "That's my dad?"

My heart stutters in my chest while I move toward him to introduce myself. Wait...*what?*

Reggie's eyes flare wide in surprise, her gaze travels from Micah to me, and I fall back against the counter. I'm pretty sure I've stopped breathing. I feel like a fragile leaf shaking in the wind, my entire body hanging onto the counter like it's the only lifeline available. My son? I need to sit down. I glance over to the kitchen table and make myself stumble to a chair. No one has said anything since that bomb was dropped, and both Reggie and Micah are looking at me like they're waiting for some kind of reaction. What did Reggie expect? A joyful greeting, hugs all around? Jesus.

I lean over, rake my hands through my hair, and tug on it in order to feel grounded. I need to say something. I *should* say something. But what? What do I say to Reggie? How could she keep something like this from me? How in the world did I end up with a son?

"Micah, honey," she begins softly. "Can you give me and Jordan a few minutes to talk?"

"Can I play on your iPad?" Micah asks eagerly. I glance to him and feel a tug deep inside my chest. How did the Universe decide I deserved a kid? Not that I can claim he's completely mine, considering I've not been around to help raise him.

"Go ahead and take it to your room, buddy. I'll come get you in a few minutes."

"Okay, Mom."

Reggie pulls a chair from the table and sits down in front of me so our knees are almost touching. I can feel the heat from her body; it's rolling off her like worried waves, crashing into my legs like unstable, sandy beaches.

"Reggie, I've got to say that I'm, well, I don't know what I am. Angry? Scared shitless? Petrified?" I'm not a crier. But right now my eyes are burning fiercely, and my breath is coming in ragged pants, so much so I can only whisper. "Why would you keep something like this from me?" And tears fall hard and fast down my cheeks.

Down...down...down...

Years of pent up grief and bitterness have collected beneath my stony exterior, making me really good at locking away emotion. *Tears.* They burn as they slip down my cheeks, each one slicing like hot knives through my flesh, cutting a path straight to my heart.

I thought I had myself under control. That I was

ready to hear it all, *know* it all. But now, things have changed—again, and I don't know anything anymore. My tears are met with Reggie's quiet sobs, and that hurts so much more. Knowing I'm the cause of her tears guts me. What am I going to do with this? *Us?*

"I'm so sorry, Jordan," Reggie sobs, covering her face with her hands. "I'm sorry I never told you, but I didn't want to hold you back. You were so talented and deserved the life you always dreamed of."

"You can't make that decision for someone else, Reggie. It wasn't fair."

"You would've stayed." She sniffs then wipes her damp cheeks with the palms of her hands. "I could never have lived with myself for holding you back."

"Still, it wasn't your decision to make. I've missed so much, Reggie. I don't know anything about him, how old he is, when his birthday is. His favorite color, anything."

Reggie laughs lightly as her entire body trembles. Her jaw shakes as though she's shivering. My girl is so nervous she's shaking like a leaf. I push off the chair, fall to my knees, kneeling in front of her. I fit perfectly here, and even on my knees we're almost eye-to-eye. My arms wrap around her waist as I pull her into my chest. Another sob escapes her rosy lips as her arms tighten around my neck.

"His birthday is on Saturday." She sniffs against the collar of my shirt, and my heart thuds harder. That's in five days. "He's going to be eight."

I have an eight-year-old son. My fingers glide through my hair and tug. Holy shit. What does an eight-year-old boy like to play with?

"You're going to have to help me out a bit when it comes to picking out a birthday gift, Reggie-bug," I say, tilting her chin up to look me in the eye. Yeah, I'm angry, hurt, and also guilty, but no kid deserves to feel unloved like my father made me feel when I was growing up. And when I love his mother like I do, there isn't going to be much standing in the way of me loving that little boy either.

Chapter 34

Reggie

Jordan's hand on my chin is warm and comforting, like a hug from someone you've missed for a very long time. I don't know why he's not screaming at me, or at the very least why he hasn't stormed out of my apartment. But then he rises a little, pulls my face to his, and his lips are on mine, crushing the guilt and fear. The kiss is his offering of slow and tender forgiveness, and I think I might just crumble to pieces for him to collect and keep in his pocket.

I'm not sure I deserve this kiss, but I'm not going to refuse it either. When he pulls away, I mourn the loss of the warmth. He pulls me to my feet, squeezes my hand, and says, "Let's go get our boy."

With his kiss, his touch, and those words, I'm returning to the gelatinous puddle of goo at Jordan's feet. He's so much more than I deserve, has so much heart he's willing to share, and I love him so stinking much.

The mood at dinner is light, relaxed even, so much so I almost forget Jordan's only known he's a father for a little over an hour. He's amazing as he talks with and teases Micah like he's one of the guys. I can only sit back and smile as they get to know each other, but before long they pull me into a game of "Did You Know?".

Jordan glances my way, a sexy smirk on his face that turns into a chuckle. "Did you know your momma has the most ticklish feet of anyone I know?" My heart melts even more at his use of the name momma.

"Yeah, even under her arms she's super ticklish," Micah answers with a giant grin.

We all go back and forth for another hour before I stand up abruptly and announce it's time for Micah to get ready for bed. Both Jordan and Micah put on mock pouty faces as I guide my boy out of the kitchen and down the hall to the bathroom. Once inside, I kneel down to talk to him.

"How are you doing, honey?" I ask, brushing the hair off his forehead. He smiles, and then hugs me fiercely around my neck.

"I like him," Micah says when he releases me from his hug. "Is he really my dad?"

"He is," I say while I nod and help him with the toothpaste. "Do you really like him?"

"Yeah." He brushes his teeth quickly, spits out the bubbles, and rinses his mouth. "Can he live with us, Mom?"

My heart swells at his innocence. He's so quick to accept Jordan; I have to wonder what it will do to him when he learns Jordan won't be around as a permanent fixture in his life. How do I explain how his daddy is a musician who travels the world performing night after night? Did I do the right thing in bringing them together?

"Let's not get ahead of ourselves, okay?" I say with a laugh. The last thing we need to do is put any unnecessary pressure on Jordan right now. Micah rushes to his bedroom, changes into pajamas, and then gives me a quick kiss when we return to the kitchen to say goodnight.

"I want Jordan to tuck me in, okay, Mom?" I glance to Jordan and my cheeks burn with embarrassment. He appears to be about as shell-shocked as one would imagine him to be.

"Honey, I don't know if he—" I say, but Jordan cuts me off.

"I'd love to tuck you in, buddy." He smiles and shoots me a quick wink. "Show me the way."

"Night, Mommy," Micah says, kissing me one more time before he bounds down the hallway to his room.

"I'm sorry," I say as Jordan snakes his arm over my shoulder and presses his lips to mine. The kiss is quick but firm, and the swipe of his tongue across my bottom lip lights a fire in my belly.

"I figure I've got about eight years to make up for," he whispers against my mouth.

If I wasn't already in love with Jordan Capshaw, I would have fallen right there. Even though I'd love to watch their exchange while Jordan tucks Micah into bed, I let them have this one moment alone. I don't know how many opportunities he'll have to do this after tonight, when he realizes who he is and what his life is like outside his break from touring.

There is no use worrying myself over what's to come. His leaving is inevitable, so instead of working myself into more tears, I tidy up the kitchen. No matter the outcome tonight, there can't be any more tears.

"So, you gonna fill me in on how I have an eight-year-old son?" Jordan says from behind me, making me jump against the counter. His tone isn't sharp or angry, but flat, as though he's resolved not to show any emotion whatsoever, and that almost hurts more than if he blew up at me for keeping him away from Micah. "Am I really as bad as my father always said I was?" A muscle in his jaw ticks, and I swear it's attached to my chest because just that little bit of worried emotion is enough to crush me. He's tried so hard his whole life to prove his father wrong, and for him to believe he's anything like that man is painful to hear.

"Jordan," I whisper while taking two steps across the kitchen floor to him. He won't look at me; in fact, he's staring at a black scuffmark on the tile floor. My hands move of their own accord, settling on his scruffy cheeks, finding strength in the fact that this man in front of me is so much stronger and better than he believes he is.

"You are nothing like your father," I whisper, urging him to look at me. When he refuses, I pull his face up. "You're a good man, Jordan Capshaw. You love with your whole heart, and even though I don't deserve it, you're offering me forgiveness

238

when you should be screaming at me."

Finally. *Finally* his light brown eyes are gazing into mine, and I feel the heat of his stare all the way down to my toes. His arms wrap around me, encapsulating me in a warm embrace. I know I shouldn't invite him to stay with me tonight, but there's nothing I want more than to feel him over me, loving me. We still have so much to talk about, but it can wait. Right now, I need to feel his love and show him all he means to me.

"You've always held my heart, Jordan." My hands travel from his cheeks to the back of his neck as I pull him closer. "When I said it had been a long time for me, I meant it. I've never been with another man. It's always been you." My cheeks burn from my admission, and when his lips meet mine, a moan travels from his mouth at the touch. His hands move from my back down to my butt as he picks me up off the floor and carries me through the apartment to my bedroom. Our lips never part as he opens the door, steps inside, and locks it behind us.

***

Over the next five days, when I'm not working, my focus is on preparing for Micah's party. Jordan has been a real help in running errands and picking up the gifts I wanted to buy for him. He even picked up something for Micah and won't tell me what it is. He says he wants it truly to be a surprise.

It's Saturday and Micah's birthday party is in full swing at the park near our apartment. There are a dozen seven- and eight-year-old boys running around, high on cupcakes and frosting, and I only hope I can keep track of them all. Stacey's here, along with Jordan, and they're both helping me wrangle the boys into a huddle so Micah can open his presents. I sit behind my son while he tears open birthday bags and wrapped gifts, and I find I can't keep my eyes off Jordan. For someone learning just a few days ago he's a father, he's sure handling it better than I could ever have hoped.

He's wearing a smile on his face that reaches his eyes, and it fills me to the brim with happiness. After we spoke more about Micah, and he told his parents about him, they demanded he take a paternity test. I have to admit it stung more than I would've thought that his parents didn't believe me. The results came back quickly, of course proving his paternity. I'm sure they'll eventually want to meet their grandson, but as of right now, there haven't been any attempts to get to know him. Jordan tells me not to worry, because he's enough for me and Micah, and deep in my heart I know he's right.

"Having a good time?" Jordan asks, startling me. His hands rest on my shoulders as he dips down to kiss my cheek, making my heart race.

"Today has been great," I answer. Actually, having him here with us has been amazing, something I never thought could happen. Now that it has, in a way it makes me sad. He's missed so much, and I can't help but wish I'd made a different choice all those years ago. But I was so young and wanted him to live his dreams.

"I want to spend the rest of the weekend with

you and Micah," he says close to my ear. "I don't want the two of you out of my sight until I have to leave on Monday to go to L.A." He squeezes my shoulders gently before sitting on the bench next to me. The heat from his body snakes around me, making me shiver in anticipation. I don't want him out of my bed the rest of the weekend.

My cheeks heat thinking about him in my bed. Never have I brought a man to my apartment, let alone had one in my bed, and I worry that Micah will catch us. By some miracle though, he's been nightmare-free and stayed in his own bed until morning each night. That is to say, both Jordan and I have agreed that for the time being, he will be gone before Micah wakes up in the morning. We don't want to confuse him right now.

Stacey's been a trooper, though, putting up with us every night. She pretends to gag every time Jordan kisses me and says she can't wait to be in her own place so she doesn't have to witness the nightly tongue wrestling. Every time she brings up moving I get a little teary-eyed, because I feel like it's the end of the Reggie and Stacey era. She's not going to be here for our nightly girl talk anymore or to tell me to grow up when I'm having a bad day.

Parents begin to show up to take their boys home, and by the time the last boy leaves I'm wiped out. The party was only two hours long, but I swear watching twelve boys ages you about five years. Stacey, Jordan, and I clean up our party area as Micah goes through his presents with gusto. Jordan gave him his present this morning, a brand new blue bike with handlebar brakes. He had the biggest

241

smile on his face until he admitted he didn't know how to ride a bike. That made me feel like the worst parent in the world, never having taught my son to ride. Jordan took it in stride, even appeared excited at the prospect of showing him the ropes.

"You ready to head home?" I ask Micah after the car is loaded and the party all cleaned up. He nods enthusiastically, turns to Jordan, and gives him his signature smile. Uh-oh, he's about to ask Jordan for the moon.

"Will you teach me how to ride my bike now?" he asks, practically jumping on the balls of his feet. Jordan beams, nods, and my boy wraps his arms around Jordan's waist like they've always belonged there. I choke back a tear, knowing I promised myself I was finished crying no matter how this turns out. I'm all in, even if that means in the end I'm all in with only Micah. I know I can't keep Jordan if he doesn't want to stay, and I won't ask him either. He needs to make that decision on his own.

Chapter 35

Jordan

Most days I still can't believe I have a son. I was royally pissed when I called my parents to tell them about Micah and my dad demanded I take a paternity test. I didn't have to take a test to know that Micah was mine. He has my eyes and, damn, that smile of his—just like mine. I like to think I'm doing a great job suppressing the hurt that sneaks up on me occasionally, but I know I'm going to have to deal with it in the long run. Holding something like this back will only blow up in my face. I'm hoping my trip to L.A. with the guys to finish our recording session will give me some clarity.

After Micah's birthday party, I did everything I could not to puff out my chest like a proud father when he asked me to teach him how to ride a bike. I haven't earned that title, not yet, but it still felt amazing to have him ask me and trust me enough to show him what to do. And let me tell you, he's an amazing kid. It didn't take him long at all to learn how to ride, and that alone filled me with pride.

Spending the nights with Reggie in her bed, loving her, holding her, makes me want things I don't know how to ask for. Maybe it's not so much the how, but the *who*. My life isn't exactly normal, and I have commitments. But they don't mean anything without Reggie and Micah. So now I'm seeking clarity.

The six of us guys are piled into the van, driving on the I-10 to L.A., and my mind won't leave Reggie and Micah. I'm never going to get the answers I want if I can't keep them off my mind. We have five days to finish these songs and make sure they're perfect. Then our break will be quickly coming to a close. Jeremy has already told the guys his plans to separate from the band and get married next month, and a large part of me wants exactly what he's getting. A family, something normal after these crazy years we've all spent together.

While Drake drives, I sit in the front seat with one foot on the dash, ear buds in, music grounding me. I always listen to the instrumental versions of our songs. It helps me focus on the tasks at hand, which right now means getting my head in the game. We have thirteen songs to finalize, and then they'll be going out to the world. I know I've said it before, but this album feels so personal, like I've stripped myself bare for the world to see who I really am. It's damn good and, when finished, will be our best release ever.

Which brings me back to Reggie. This album feels like my farewell. The goodbye my fans need and deserve.

***

Two days of being in the studio makes me feel like a caged animal. Our rhythm is off, the sound isn't right, and no matter what I do I can't find the heart to get the job done. Mandy Montrose, our agent, stands behind the glass with her arms folded across her chest, glaring at me. She's already called me out once today to give me the "talk," but I just can't pull it together. I'm screwing this up for everyone, and right now the look Mandy's giving me says she's one minute away from screaming.

"Jordan!" Well, that minute flew by quickly. "Get your ass out here," she growls over the speakers. The guys shake their heads as I leave the microphone. "Go to lunch, guys," Mandy says, dismissing the band. When I step through the door, she's there on the other side with her face pinched in anger. Her white blouse is wrinkled over her chest from crossing her arms all morning.

"You've been in studio for nearly two days, Jordan, and we haven't been able to produce music worth the toilet paper to wipe my ass. What is wrong with you?" She turns, her artificially black hair swishing over her shoulder as she paces across the small waiting room. Four barely padded chairs line the short wall, and opposite is another glass divider that looks into the sound room. The walls are gray with framed gold and platinum records hanging sporadically around the seven-by-ten room.

Is it wrong that, although I know these songs are amazing and the album will be incredible, I suddenly don't really care to get them out to the world? Which brings me to a phone call I need to make. And fast.

I pull my cell from my pocket, holding up a finger to silence her, and begin scrolling through my contacts. When I find the name I'm looking for and walk out of the waiting room, Mandy follows close behind, mumbling a string of swear words. When I hit the cement outside the studio, I breathe a sigh of relief. Well, maybe not quite relief, more like a breath of hope. Meaning I sure hope I know what I'm doing.

"Where the hell are you going?" she demands, wrinkling the blouse even more. "You are contractually obligated to record this album! You can't just walk away from our conversation." She's practically screaming now, standing outside the studio for anyone within twenty yards to hear.

"I'm taking a lunch break," I say, readying to hail a taxi. "Let's meet early tomorrow, and you'll get your album." Her jaw drops as I quickly jump into a cab that just pulled up. Before she has time to react, I slap the driver on the shoulder and tell him I'm ready to go. He quirks a smile, nods, and then drives away from the curb, leaving Mandy wearing a scowl. Palming my cell, I press *send* and wait for the line to pick up.

"I haven't heard from you in almost two years," Greg Bryant, my lawyer, says in his deep baritone voice. "How the hell are you doing? Wait. Don't answer that. Why are you calling me?"

I've known Greg for several years; actually, he's been my lawyer since White Shadow signed our record deal. He's what the music industry would consider a hard-ass in the business. He knows his shit, and I wasted no time in putting him on retainer when we signed our contract.

"I'm here in L.A., and I need a favor," I say with a chuckle. "I need you to look over my contract with Mandy Montrose and Orion Records and tell me how ironclad it is."

A long pause hangs on the line before he says anything. "What's this all about, Jordan?"

"I want to retire, and I need to know how long I've got before I can do it."

"Wow. I'm not in the office, but if you want to meet me there in an hour, we can go over it."

"Sure, I'll see you in an hour."

Forty-five minutes later, I'm outside the building where Greg's office is located on the twenty-ninth floor, overlooking a large man-made lake near the center of the city. Why the city developers thought they needed to build a lake right here is beyond me. I ride the elevator up and stare out the glass windows as the people get smaller and smaller the higher I go. When the elevator doors open, Greg is waiting for me, wearing a pair of plaid golf shorts and a pale blue Polo shirt. His muddy brown hair is styled into a messy look, not unlike the one every guy tries to create to make the world think they spend no time at all on their hair.

"I never pictured you as a golfer, Greg," I say as we shake hands. "I figured more of a tennis player."

"Actually, I play both." He smirks and leads me to his office. He offers me a Cuban cigar when I sit down across from him, but I turn it down. "So, what brought on your sudden desire to cut out of the music industry?" he asks as he turns on his computer.

"Would you believe love?"

His eyes widen, but he smiles and pulls up my contracts with Mandy and the record label.

"She must be something to make the one and only Jordan Capshaw want to give up touring and all the girls throwing themselves at your feet."

Greg scans through the contracts, scribbles some notes on a piece of paper, and then prints off a couple pages. I take a moment to watch him as he reads through the pages he printed one more time. His lips purse, then relax, and he shakes his head, humming quietly to himself.

His office is made up of windows on two sides that overlook the lake below, while the other two walls are a rich, navy blue and give the room a moody glow. A painting of a massive oak tree reminds me of the large trees lining the driveway of Jemma's home. Or rather, the house and land I now own. I only bought it because it was the start of my recovery, and I can't help but wonder now if it will be my last stop on this journey called life.

Greg looks up from the papers with a surprised look on his face. I can't tell if this is a good sign or not.

"Well, it looks like your contract is pretty solid," he says, and my heart drops to the floor. "They covered all their bases. If you'd come to me three months ago, I would've said there's no way you could break the contract."

A whoosh of air rushes from my lungs. "So you're saying what, exactly?"

"First, it would seem your contract with Orion Records is complete." A smile tugs at his lips as he leans back in his chair.

"So, this new album Mandy has us recording doesn't even have a home to go to right now?"

Greg shakes his head and continues. "It would also seem that Mandy Montrose's contract as White Shadow's agent expires next month."

"What does this all mean?" I ask, hoping I'm understanding correctly.

"It means that you and White Shadow are only bound by the terms of Mandy Montrose's contract for another twenty-eight days. You will be free agents and can seek new representation or retire or do whatever you want."

There has to be a catch. No one gets this lucky; something's not adding up. "It's not that I don't trust your legal skills, Greg, but how did this get by Mandy? Why hasn't she brought up renewing our contract? What if I didn't want out and the album was cut and ready to go?"

"If you truly want out, now is your chance. I'm not sure I'd be questioning the how and why if I were you." Greg's advice is legit, but I can't help but feel there's something he's missing. Luck just hasn't ever been on my side.

"All right, man. If you say we're free in a month, then I'm going to take your word for it." I can't believe this weight has been lifted from my shoulders. We shake hands, and I'm so relieved I could skip down the hall, to the elevator, and all the way back to the hotel if it weren't so far away. This is the best news I could've received, and now I can meet up with the guys and figure out what to do from here.

I dial Mandy on my cell and make some random excuse about being unable to show up tomorrow to finish the album and offer an apology for walking out on her earlier. It was rude and I shouldn't have done it. Though the end result is better than I could have hoped for.

I'm meeting the guys back at the hotel to discuss the future of the band, but first I send a quick text to Reggie letting her know my plans might be changing. I hate to stay away longer, but after tonight my life may be changing even more drastically than it already has.

Jeremy slaps me on my shoulder in a greeting when I walk through Drake's hotel room. The guys are all sitting around the small table playing a round of poker and it makes me happy to see these guys who are like brothers to me.

"What's up, bro?" Carson asks, pulling the discarded cards into a pile in front of him. "Mandy was royally pissed when you walked out today."

I rake my hands through my hair, smile, and plop down on the edge of the bed. "Yeah, that was a really dick move on my part. I called her and apologized."

"You okay?" Drake asks after taking a swig from a bottle of water.

There really isn't any way to ease in to what my plans are, so I lay it all out for them to see like the deck of cards in front of Carson.

"Our contract with the label is complete," I say, releasing a breath. The guys stare at me in confusion. "Mandy's contract as our agent expires in a month and I'm giving you my notice. You're going to need to find a new front man for White Shadow."

There is a stilled silence in the room as the guys glance back and forth between us all. A smile grows on Jeremy's face and then as if the weight of the room shifts, Drake stands and reaches for my hand.

"It's about damn time you came to your senses and married that girl," he says, smiling so wide that creases form on the outer edges of his eyes.

"Who said anything about getting hitched?" I ask with a grin overtaking my own face.

"This guy over here is tying the knot next month," Drake says, pointing over his shoulder at JD. "It was only a matter of time before you followed suit. Though we all think it should have been you first."

"Hey!" Jeremy says with a smirk. "When you know, you know." He shrugs and the rest of the night is like this. Easy, casual, and the way family should be.

Chapter 36

Reggie

Stacey is moving out today, and I'm an emotional wreck. Micah is upset and won't talk to me, and Jordan's been MIA for so long it scares me. I receive a random text from him every once in a while, but it feels like his trip to L.A. was a goodbye. If it wasn't, then why hasn't he come back to me? I know his recording session is done, and he should've been home five days ago.

I shake my head and return my focus to Stacey, who's packing the last of the boxes with the remaining items from her bedroom. Her brother, James, and two of his friends showed up an hour ago and are loading up a small U-Haul truck with her large furniture. Her bedroom is empty except for some boxes lining one wall, and it hits me this really is the end of the Reggie and Stacey show.

"Are you sure you want to do this?" I ask, hoping she's considering changing her mind. "You don't have to move out."

Stacey plops to the floor, sits cross-legged, and blows out a breath. Her red hair is pulled up into a messy knot on the top of her head, and it reminds me of the day we moved in together all those years ago. This complex isn't the nicest, but it's housed us for almost nine years. Nothing is going to be the same when she's gone.

"It's time for me to be on my own, Reggie," she says quietly. "I need to find out who I really am. You know this. Please don't make this harder on me than it already is. I need to know you're going to be okay when I'm gone."

I try to laugh it off, play it like I've got this. The truth is I'm terrified of living on my own. I've been able to rely on Stacey whenever I've needed her, and her moving out feels like a divorce. I'm going to officially be a single parent, and I don't have any idea how to do that.

"You know Micah and I will be fine," I say, lying through my teeth. I know she needs to do this; technically we both need this. It doesn't mean I have to like it.

We work together to finish the last of her packing as the boys come into her room and lug the boxes to the U-Haul. When the last of her things are loaded, I stare at her empty room with fondness. So many nights that ended with sleepovers, like we were still teenagers.

"Ready?" Stacey says, pulling me into a hug. I nod and follow her down the stairs, where I find Micah sitting in the middle of the seat in the U-Haul cab. Even though he won't talk to me because he thinks it's my fault she's leaving, he still wants to be a part of Stacey's big move. He loves her just as much as I do, and I know this is just as hard on him as it is me.

James's friends, Drew and Harley, slide into the truck, sitting on either side of Micah, and start up the engine. James is driving Stacey's car, and she's riding with me to her new place. When we arrive, the look on Stacey's face is pure joy. I do my best to mimic her excitement as I follow her to her new apartment. The guys begin unloading boxes and stacking them in the second bedroom. While they are unloading, Stacey and I clean the kitchen, readying for her things. An hour into unloading, there's a knock on the door, followed by a distinct "Hello?" that makes my stomach drop.

I peek around the door to see Jordan holding a stack of pizza boxes, and he's dressed in a pair of jeans and a vintage, gray Pearl Jam t-shirt. He smiles as he walks into the apartment, leans down, pressing a kiss to my cheek, and sets the pizzas on the counter.

"What are you doing here?" I ask, wiping the sweat from my forehead with the back of my hand.

"I brought pizza," he says with a killer smirk that makes my lady parts swoon. Not that there will be any swooning in the near future. I'm mad at him for ignoring me for so long.

"I can see that," I say, tossing the wet dishrag into the sink. "But why are you here?"

"Stacey mentioned everyone would be hungry after moving her things when I talked to her yesterday, so I decided to show up. With food." He talked to *her* and not me? Why? He's leaning against the kitchen counter, arms folded over his chest, looking as good as ever. Which doesn't make seeing him here any easier.

"But why now? You haven't bothered to call or to stop by since L.A. Why is that?"

He shrugs as a smile tugs at his lips. "Missed me, did you?"

Groaning in frustration, I grab the four boxes of pizza and look around Stacey's kitchen for somewhere to put them. Obviously, where Jordan set them is perfectly fine, but it feels like he's won whatever this is and had the last word. I place them about six inches to the right of where they were, breeze past him, and call out from the living room that food is here. Within seconds, the three guys are barreling toward me with Stacey in tow.

I push past the guys and Jordan, and a hand clasps around my elbow, pulling me into Jordan's chest. He smells so good, like heat and musk and hot summer nights. "I didn't get back to Phoenix until last night," he says, brushing his lips against my cheek.

"And you didn't think to call me while you extended your stay in L.A.?" His hands glide down my sides, stopping at the top of my jeans. He slides his fingers through my belt loops and pulls me closer.

"I had some things I needed to take care of before I came back to you and Micah. Now that they're done, I'm back and can't wait to spend the rest of my life loving you and our son."

Yes, I still melt when I hear him refer to Micah this way, and I think I always will. But I can't live in a melty kind of world; I need to live in the real world where the man I love is here to stay. I won't let him come in and out of our lives, because it's too hard. Thinking about him constantly traveling, only coming home to me and Micah every few months, hurts like a spoon digging through my chest, trying to find my heart.

"Jordan, you can't just waltz into my life whenever you want. There's too much at stake, and it'll only end up hurting all three of us in the end." I pull away from the warmth of his body and return to the sink for the dishrag. I need to finish cleaning up the kitchen.

"So, you're going to push me away before we even try to be a family? Before you hear me out?" Jordan steels his gaze, and it shoots through me like a harpoon. It cuts deep, anchoring us together, making it impossible to truly let him go.

"I want you to choose us, Jordan," I say with a whimper. "I want all-inclusive love, and for you to hold me each and every night and never let me go. I want you to tuck our son in at night, tell him you love him and will always be here with us. I want you now and forever." My cheeks burn at how selfish I sound, but I need to be honest with him. He needs to know exactly what I want, because I'm not willing to compromise any longer. "Can you do that, Jordan? Can you be all in with me?"

His shoulders are shaking, and he's slowly moving his head side to side. He's smiling, holding back a laugh.

"You're laughing?" I say incredulously. "What part of what I said do you find humorous, exactly?"

My defenses are raised and I fold my arms across my chest.

"Bug," he says as he closes the short distance between us. "I'm all in. Have been since the day I told you I love you." Jordan's hands come to rest on my shoulders, and his thumbs traces lines up and down the sides of my throat. His touch sends sparks pinging through my body.

"But what does that mean? I need to know." Men are so hard to decipher. I just want him to tell me everything I want to hear.

"It means I love you, and I want to spend the rest of my life making you and Micah happy." His arms engulf me in a firm embrace, and I settle against his chest. This is home, this is comfort, right where my heart belongs—in the capable hands of Jordan Capshaw.

We spend the rest of the afternoon helping Stacey unpack and settle in, and then Jordan follows me and Micah back to my apartment. Micah crashes the minute he's buckled in the backseat, and I'm more than wiped out myself. Jordan carries our boy to bed, tucks him in, and walks me to my bedroom. He pulls off my shirt, pops the button of my jeans, and slowly slides them off my legs. He presses a warm kiss to my forehead and then steps back, admiring my state of undress. His eyes rake over me, making my entire body light on fire with want.

His lips turn up into a crooked smile as he leaves the room. I stand in the middle of the bedroom in my bra and panties, wondering why he disappeared. From the bathroom I hear the water turn on in the tub and the rustling noises of him searching my cabinets. Moment later, he returns, his eyes still roving over my body.

"Go relax in the bathtub," he says with another soft kiss to my forehead. "You've had a stressful day, and you're exhausted. Let me take care of you tonight." He guides me out of my room and into the bathroom, where he watches hungrily as I slip off my panties and unclip my bra, letting it slip to the floor. His Adam's apple bobs, and it makes me feel amazing knowing this man still wants me after all these years apart. That even after having his child, he still finds me desirable. And I want him just as much.

***

I feel like I have a hangover from hell. My insides have all but twisted inside out and are crawling their way out of my throat. I haven't been sick like this in years. Poor Micah has been stuck in front of the TV for two days since I can hardly get out of bed.

"Mom?" he cries from the living room. "Mom!"

I can barely move, but when my boy needs me, I have to go to him. Groaning, I manage to slip out of bed and stumble down the hallway. Micah is huddled up on the couch with two blankets wrapped around his little body.

"Are you sick, buddy?" I ask and run my hand over his forehead. He's burning up, leaving no doubt he's got what I have—the flu. Shit. I can't call Stacey to come stay with us, because she's working, and my parents are too far away, not that I want them to be here right now. We're on our own, I guess.

We sit together on the couch, watching *Spongebob Squarepants* until late in the night. I've drifted off to sleep, only to be woken up by Micah groaning and holding his stomach. He belches, and with it comes a spray of vomit that lands on the carpet in front of him. I didn't even have time to grab him a bucket. I glance at the clock. It's almost 2 a.m., and I don't know what else to do but call Jordan. I need help, and I need it now.

After the second time I call, he answers. "Hello?" His voice is gravelly and full of late night grogginess.

"We're sick with the plague, and I need you," is all I say before I hang up and try to figure out where to begin cleaning up the mess in the living room. If he really wants us, then this is what he's going to get.

Chapter 37

Jordan

Reggie answers the door wearing a stained tank top and a pair of old, red plaid boxers. Her hair is matted to her head, and she holds a tissue to her nose. In her other hand she's gripping a rag and a spray bottle of some kind, and my heart nearly leaps out of my chest with the urge to embrace her. Damn, she's a mess, but she's beautiful despite being sick.

"This is it," she says, though it comes out as more of a sob. "You want this? I've got puke to clean up in the living room. I smell like ass, look like I've been run over by a truck hauling manure, and I feel like death." She gestures to her body, her house, and then her head falls to her chest as though she's calling it quits.

"My life isn't glamorous, and shit hits the fan when I get sick." A laugh bubbles from her throat as she glances around the room, taking in the state of things. "I've never done this single mom thing. I've always had Stacey, and now she's gone."

Tears pool in the corners of her eyes as she sniffs and runs a tissue over her cheeks. I step into her apartment, close the door, and pull her into my arms, tucking her head to my chest. The skin on her forehead is burning up, and she really doesn't smell all that good—but I don't care. I bring my lips to the top of her head and give her a quick kiss. These past couple weeks without her have been some of my worst. I know we have shit to figure out; I have a son I hardly know. But he's mine—and *hers*—and that's all I need to know. For once in my life I want more of those little things running and calling me Daddy.

My fingers glide under Reggie's chin and bring her head up to look me in the eyes. I'm done hiding what's in my heart, and I'm done letting her push me away.

"Reggie-bug," I begin, but she closes her eyes tightly as though she doesn't want to hear what I have to say. It breaks my heart. "Bug, look at me." She shakes her head, pulls her lips between her teeth, and clamps her eyes harder.

"Jordan, please don't," she whispers.

"Regina Mariquita Velasco, don't you push me away. I'm here at two in the morning for you—will *always* be here for you. I want you sick and smelling like ass and feeling like death. And puke all over the living room floor. I want you and Micah no matter what you look like. I'm not going anywhere, ever again."

Reggie's shoulders are shaking in my arms as tears slip down her pale cheeks. I bend forward and claim her mouth with mine, giving her a quick kiss, not caring that she's sick. When I pull away, her eyes are wide, and her mouth hangs open.

"I haven't brushed my teeth in three days," she admits.

I shrug, grab her by the shoulders, and turn her around. "Go to bed. I've got this," I say, giving her a little shove and smacking her ass lightly. She walks down the hall, and I swear I can see the weight fall off her shoulders as she closes her bedroom door.

I take a look around Reggie's apartment and, for a moment, allow myself to panic just a little. The place is a wreck. Micah is groaning from the couch, holding a bucket in his hands while watching some cartoons on the television. My palms begin to sweat as I prepare to throw myself into the fire with this boy—my son. I wonder if he will ever like me. Can I be the father he deserves? I sure didn't have a great example of a father, so at least I know if I don't follow his footsteps, I have a fighting chance.

I step around the puddle of vomit and sit next to Micah on the couch. His face is pale, but his cheeks are bright pink from fever, just like his mom's. I cup my hand over his forehead, and he's hot too.

"How you feeling, little man?" I ask. Micah shrugs, and the blanket he has over his shoulders slips down, so I pull it back up and tuck it around him again. "What are you doing up so late?"

"I got sick and can't go back to sleep yet," he says as he burps and brings the bucket up to his face before puking again. I cringe and clench my teeth, trying hard not to lose it.

When he finishes, his eyes are bloodshot and watering. What did my mom do when I was sick? I try to remember a time when I was younger, and then it comes to me. I remember! I rub his back for a minute and ask for his bucket. I dump the contents into the toilet, wash it out, and rush it back to him in case he has a repeat episode.

"I'm going to bring you some soda crackers and a glass of water, okay?" Micah nods and returns his focus to the TV. In the kitchen I find a box of saltine crackers, and I fill a sandwich bag with a few and then bring Micah some water.

"Don't eat if you're not hungry. If you are, only eat one cracker at a time. We don't want you throwing up what you just ate."

Okay. I can do this. Micah seems to be doing all right, Reggie's sleeping, and all I need to do now is clean up the mess on the carpet. I search through the apartment until I find the supplies I need and then get to work. Twenty minutes later, the carpet is clean, though I think I will call a carpet cleaner in the morning to come wash them anyway, otherwise the place might begin to really smell. I wash my hands and begin cleaning up the rest of the apartment, starting with the dishes in the kitchen. Around four in the morning, Micah is feeling a little better and asks me to take him to bed.

For a moment, I'm stuck standing next to the couch as Micah stares up at me, his brown eyes having a hard time staying open. He hasn't thrown up since the last time, but as we walk down the hall to his room, I carry his bucket just in case. He climbs in bed and scoots next to the wall and pats the space next to him.

"Will you read to me?" he asks, his eyes blinking rapidly as though he's fighting to keep them open.

"Sure. What would you like me to read?" He points to a book on his dresser, *Jacob Wonderbar and the Cosmic Space Kapow*. I sit down next to Micah on his twin bed and open to the page he has dog-eared. About three paragraphs into Jacob getting kidnapped by space pirates, Micah is fast asleep.

Chapter 38

Reggie

The first thing I notice when I return to the planet of the living is my clean apartment. Clean as in dishes are done, the counters are clean, pillows are organized, and best of all, Micah's vomit is cleaned up. My heart swells knowing Jordan must have been up really late taking care of my house and our son. As quickly as my heart swells, just saying *our son* makes it skip two beats.

Our conversation at the door last night halts me in my tracks. He said he's not leaving again. *Again.* What does that mean? Tear prick at my eyes, but I quickly wipe them away and walk down the hall to Micah's room. His room is dark, but I don't need to turn the light on to see the sight across the small room. My breath catches in my throat. I should walk away, but I can't. The damned tears break free regardless of how much I wipe them away.

Lying in the bed is Jordan with his arm under my boy, who is tucked into his side lying with his head on his father's chest. My chest constricts, and the love I feel for them both nearly explodes out of me. Are we all going to be okay? Can we really be a family after all of this?

I turn to leave the room, but Jordan whispers across the way, "Hey. How are you feeling?"

A smile parts my lips as I sniff away my tears and nod. "Better, thanks to you."

Jordan shifts, scooting Micah off of him, returning my boy back to bed as he pulls the blankets over his sleeping form. He stands and stretches, crosses the room, and places his hand on my lower back as we close the door and walk across the hall to my room. We sit apart on the edge of my bed, with our hands linked between us. The silence drags on and I can feel the heavy weight of Jordan's gaze on me, but I don't know what to do or what he wants. So I do what I do best, fill the awkwardness with small talk.

"I really want to thank you for coming over last night. I can't tell you how much I appreciate it." My fingers tug on the hem of my shorts, which are clean now that I've showered and washed my hair. "And the apartment, you didn't have to clean it."

"What are you doing, Bug?" Jordan asks as he slips to his knees in front of me. "What part of what I said last night isn't getting through your thick skull? Was it the part where I said I didn't care if you were sick? Or when I said I didn't care if you smelled? Which, by the way, as much as I *didn't* care that you smelled, I really love how you smell now. You smell like vanilla and spice, and it makes me want to lick every inch of your skin."

His hands close over my thighs, eyes searching mine, and I want so badly to fully give him my heart. I know what I feel for him, what I want from him, and how badly I long for him to stay in my life. He must see the hesitation on my face, because his hands fall to his sides and the muscles in his jaw clench as he closes his eyes and turns his head.

"Damn," he says as he stands, places a kiss on my forehead, and walks out of my bedroom. Within seconds, I hear the snick of the front door closing and the cracking of my heart. It's not small, in fact it's so wide I could crawl inside and be lost forever in the chasm I just created by hesitating. He walked away and I didn't stop him. I don't understand what we're doing to each other. He loves me—I know this. Why did I not stop him? Why did he walk away?

"Mom?" Micah's now standing at my door, rubbing the sleep from his eyes. I pull him in for a hug, and the tears just fall. I can't stop them, and when Micah's arms hug me tightly I choke on my sobs.

"Where did Dad go?"

A gasp is pulled from my chest. He called Jordan his dad. What happened last night that my boy decided he could trust Jordan enough to call him his father? What is wrong with me that I didn't say the things Jordan needed to hear? I'm such a fool. He's gone, probably patting himself on the back for getting out of my crazy life before it was too late.

"How are you feeling, buddy?" I run my hands over his head, feeling for a temperature, but he feels normal. "Did Jordan take care of you last night?"

Micah nods, and a smile spreads across his face. "He read *Jacob Wonderbar* to me and then fell asleep in my bed."

"I saw that, honey." We've read all three books in the series, and whenever we finish them he always asks to start over. "Is your tummy still feeling icky?"

"No. Dad gave me crackers and water last night while he cleaned up my puke."

There's a glow inside my chest; it's warm and bright, and like a magnet it's pulling me off the bed and toward the front door. I have to see if by any chance he's still in the parking lot.

"Micah, honey…Mommy will be right back, okay? I need to go outside for a second." I kiss his forehead, pull a sweatshirt over my head, and jog out of the room. I reach for the doorknob of the front door, but it twists on its own and swings inward, making me step back.

"Jordan." His name is a whisper on my lips, a prayer in my soul.

"I forgot my shoes in Micah's room." I glance at his feet to find him wearing only a pair of white socks with dirty soles from walking through the parking lot. He steps around me with his head lowered and jaw closed tight.

What am I doing? I was just going to find him, and now I've let him breeze by me. Panicking. That's what I'm doing. He's walking toward me now, shoes in hand, and his eyes are focused on the door behind me.

Block his way. My body reacts, doing what my brain hasn't yet caught up to.

"Reggie-bug, I need you to step out of my way," he warns, his voice low and soft.

I shake my head and press my back against the door. "I don't want you to leave." Words. The words have finally arrived, thank goodness. Jordan cocks a brow and tilts his head a fraction. "I want you to stay."

Jordan's lids close halfway, he clenches his jaw, and sighs heavily through his nose. His shoulders slump and then he says, "I won't stay here if you don't feel the same way I do. Do you not feel this?" He grasps my hand and places it over his rapidly beating heart and closes his eyes. When they open, they're glossy, the rims of his lids are bright pink. I'm breaking his heart even though I'm trying to give him all of mine. I shake my head as my own tears build and slip down my cheeks.

There's no other way to say what I need without taking a deep breath. Inhale, exhale. "I've loved you for eleven years. I've never stopped even though I tried. I tried so hard to forget you. When we were fifteen, I knew you were it for me. Eleven years later, you're still the one."

I pause to take another deep breath. Jordan's eyes haven't left mine since I started talking, and his thoughts are hidden well on his face.

"I love you, Jordan Capshaw. I love your heart, your courage, and strength. I love that you want to be a father to my son. *Our* son. He has called you Dad all morning, and there's nothing sweeter I could ever hear. I love you, and I need you to stay. To love me."

The dull thud of a pair of heavy shoes fills the

silence, and Jordan's hands cup my cheeks as he pulls my mouth to his. His lips cover mine, his tongue invades my mouth, and everything feels complete. My arms twine together behind Jordan's neck as the kiss grows desperate, like a deep hunger that can't be satisfied by this one kiss.

"Dad!" Micah runs to us, and I choke on a sob at the way my boy wraps his arms around us. This is what life should be—warm hugs, passionate kisses, and hearts running over with love from a good man and our little boy.

After Jordan tucks Micah in for the night, I greet him at the door with a contented smile. My heart is at peace, and I feel like my life is complete. Everything is right with us now, and together, the three of us will be the family I always hoped we could be, but never thought we'd become. His hands squeeze the tops of my shoulders and slide down my arms, stopping at my hands. He twines his fingers with mine and pulls me into the bedroom. We topple onto the mattress, still holding hands and quietly laughing like our worries have disappeared.

"Bug," he says, pulling one of my hands to his lips. Jordan kisses my knuckles one by one and then rests my hand over his heart. "There are some things I need to tell you."

My eyes bug out, making him laugh. "I don't know if I can handle it," I say, pulling away from his touch. He reaches out, grips my waist with his large hands, and rolls on top of me. Heat rises to my cheeks, my hair fans over the bed, and he looks at me like he knows one kiss won't be enough. But he does it anyway. His lips are warm and hesitant on mine, but as soon as his tongue crosses into my mouth, my resistance fades faster than water on a hot sidewalk in the middle of July.

My legs move around his, pulling him down against my pelvis. I want more, though I shouldn't right now since Jordan's trying to have a serious conversation with me. He breaks our kiss, brushes the hair away from my face, and pushes up from me so he's resting on his elbows over me.

"Some things came up in L.A. and I need to run a couple things by you," he says slowly, dragging this on longer than necessary.

I squirm beneath him, readying for the shoe to drop. "What things?" I ask, my voice cracking.

"Good things. At least I think they are." He scrunches his nose like he's trying to guess what I have to say. When I say nothing, he continues.

"The guys and I need to go back to L.A. to finish recording the album."

My brows draw together. "I thought you already finished it."

He shakes his head, kisses the tip of my nose, and continues. "My contract with the record label is up." I quietly gasp and hold my breath—I will break if he's telling me he has to leave. "My agent's contract expires in a month. The guys and I are going to head back to L.A., finish the album, and then I'm out. I'm retiring."

I slowly release the breath I was holding and like it was the one thing keeping me from giving all of myself to Jordan, a dam breaks loose. I close my eyes, greedily take his lips with mine, and kiss him like there's no tomorrow. We're a tangle of limbs,

271

grasping at the future, neither one of us willing to let go. Ever again.

"You're done? You're really done?" I ask with a squeal when we break apart.

He nods and then, like it's casual conversation, he tells me about the house on a ranch he bought in Washington he wants me to see.

"This house is where I first gave sobriety a chance and it means a lot to me," he says, rolling off and away from me. "This house is the reason I didn't come back here right away after L.A. There were a few things that needed to be repaired before I take you and Micah up there to see it. But I really think you'll love it there."

I don't know where we'll end up, if we'll pack up and move to this ranch of his, but I can't wait to go with him and Micah there so he can show me how his journey back to me began.

Epilogue

Eighteen Months Later

Jordan

I hate the smell of hospitals. Bleach, antiseptic, blaring beeping noises, and the constant clicking of closing doors grates on my nerves. That sound is like someone chewing gum and popping bubbles in your ears over and over. I don't know how Reggie can concentrate with the smells and sounds.

Her hand squeezes around mine, and the doctor between her legs tells her to bear down and push. Her cheeks puff out, face turns bright red, and she closes her eyes so tight even her inky lashes disappear.

"I can see the head," Dr. Robertson says with an easy grin. "Would you like to touch it?"

That would be a resounding no on my part, though I glance at Reggie, who shakes her head violently.

"Here's comes another one. You're doing great.

One last big push and you should get to meet your baby."

Reggie takes a deep breath and begins to push again.

"Keep pushing," the nurse urges her while nodding.

"Come on, Reggie, you can do this." Dr. Robertson glances up at us as the contraction stops briefly.

"I can't!" Reggie growls. "I want an epidural!"

The doctor laughs and shakes his head. "Too late for that, Reggie." He pauses, glances at the monitor, and says, "Okay, give it all you've got, Reggie. This one should do it."

I lean in close to Reggie to tell her I love her and give her the encouragement she needs. I kiss her damp forehead as she bears down, pushing, until the doctor slides back holding a tiny pink thing squirming in his hands.

"Looks like a healthy baby girl," Doctor Robertson says as he hands her to the nurses who quickly pat her with blankets and then bring her over Reggie's stomach.

"You can cut the cord," the nurse says, holding out a pair of medical scissors.

I shake my head and instead study this tiny infant being cleaned quickly and now placed in my wife's arms. Reggie's eyes are misty and she slides the shoulder of her gown down and brings the baby to her breast. Her tiny lips part and she begins nursing right away.

I thought I knew what love was. I thought having Reggie's love was enough. But that day Micah wrapped Reggie and me in a hug and he called me Dad, I could've cried. Okay, a stray tear might have fallen, but I swiped it away before anyone noticed. *But now*. This moment, as our baby girl nurses at Reggie's breast, my heart swells with more love than I ever knew I was capable of. Reggie looks more beautiful than I've ever seen her, as though she has a glow surrounding her and the baby. *Our baby*.

"You want to hold her?" Reggie asks.

I nod, unable to contain the grin on my face. Reggie slips a finger into the baby's mouth to break the suction and lays her gently into my arms. Her little eyes flicker open, her cheek twitches, and then she promptly falls asleep.

"What are we going to name her?" I whisper, and then sit in the chair beside the bed. When we found out Reggie was pregnant, we decided not to find out the baby's gender. We talked about names, but never settled on one, boy or girl.

Reggie's lips twist to the side as she studies our baby girl. "Annie?"

Annie. Annie Capshaw. "I like it. Annie Mariquita Capshaw. My little ladybug."

While the nurses clean up Annie and Reggie, I head to the waiting room where Micah is with Vic and Jemma. A year and a half ago, after talking with my lawyer and the band, we finished and released the album then walked away as a group. We called the album *Farewell* and it went double platinum. Carson and Drake still play together at local shows pretty regularly, but I'm done. I want my family and don't want to be on the road anymore. Even though the guys understood, they wanted me to think about it before making a final decision, though I didn't have to do any thinking at all. My decision had been made I think even before I knew about Micah. But he sealed the deal. I wanted to be there to raise my son in whatever capacity Reggie wanted or needed. Thankfully she wanted *me*.

After Jeremy and Emily's wedding, we talked a lot about staying in Phoenix, but after I told Reggie about the house in Washington, she and Micah both wanted to see it. We flew up in May after Micah finished school, and Reggie fell in love with the land and house, so we packed up and moved in June. Jemma and Reggie instantly became friends, not that I didn't think they wouldn't. And in July we were married under the giant trees on the ranch. We flew back to Phoenix in November when Emily had her baby boy she and JD named Bryce. I knew I wanted to make babies with Reggie the minute I saw Jeremy holding his son.

Now, Jemma and Vic sit with my boy in the hospital waiting room with their own little girl who is sleeping in her stroller. Jemma's about to pop again any day now with another girl, which I know will make Reggie happy knowing Annie will have a friend right away.

"How is she?" Jemma asks as she pushes herself up from the chair. A smile takes over my face as I hug Micah and ask them all if they want to meet Annie. They follow me through the hallway and back to Reggie's room. She's sitting up in bed, holding our little bug, and beaming. God, she's beautiful.

Micah runs to his mother, softly strokes the black hair on Annie's head, and smiles up at us. "She's so tiny," he says quietly.

We all laugh and visit until Izzy, Vic and Jemma's daughter, wakes up and begins to cry.

"Let's take her home," Jemma says. She wraps me in a quick hug and then whispers in my ear, "You did good, Jordan. So good."

And I feel it. This is the life I've always wanted. It's full of love, laughter, and wonder. I've made mistakes in my life—huge mistakes—but I like to believe the changes I've made and the paths I took led me to where I am today. And I'm overwhelmingly happy, to the point where my addictions no longer rule my life. I'm no longer tied to them, worrying about dark corners and easy escapes. I'm whole. I'm better.

As Annie falls asleep on Reggie's chest, I lean down, kiss my wife's lips, and whisper in her ear. "Let's make more of these."

The End

Raining Down Release

CHAPTER 1

July

Stacey

It's hot as hell and I'm sweating in places I never knew could sweat until moving here when I was twelve. Whoever decided to settle in Phoenix back in the day was a complete and utter lunatic. A hundred and thirteen degrees and we still haven't hit our summer peak.

I hate the summers here.

I especially hate the fact that the apartment complex I live in doesn't have a pool. You know what else I hate? My apartment and the neighbors who smoke more weed than is medically necessary, if you know what I mean. To top it off, the vents in my place are somehow directly linked to their pot-filled living room and I'm pretty sure I go to work every day partially stoned.

Which is altogether strange, because the few times I actually smoked pot in high school, it made me feel like I loved everyone. Can you develop an allergy to weed? One that comes with bitter rage that strikes at any hour of the day, especially when you least expect it?

Like today.

In front of my boss.

That was fun.

My neighbor's pot addiction better not get me fired from my job. Speaking of weed, an actual plume of smoke just wafted through the stinking vent over my head. What the heck? This has got to stop before I have a freaking meltdown. Remote in hand, I press pause on *The Walking Dead*, jump to my feet, and climb on top of the back of my brown chenille couch and peer through the vent. I can seriously see right into their living room.

"Hey!" I shout, pounding on the dusty metal vent. Three sets of heads glance around the room trying to find the source of my voice. "Up here, jackasses." One of them stands, turns, and meets me at the wall. Swallowing back a little bit of fear when I catch a slight glance at his tatted up face, I say, "You guys are smoking me out over here. Could you please move to another room to get high?"

The guy laughs, turning his head toward his buddies, who also burst into laughter. "Dude, give me the reefer," scary tattooed guy says. He turns back to me, joint in hand, and brings it to his mouth. Before I have time to back away or process what he's doing, he blows a long puff of smoke through the vent. It hits me square in the face, making my eyes tear up and my lungs constrict, sending me into a coughing fit.

The guy and his friends' laughter sends chills down my spine as I recover. My head spins a little, so I sit back on the couch and press *play* on the remote. I have got to find a way out of this lease. On the plus side, the zombies on *The Walking Dead* are starting to look hot. So maybe I'm not allergic to weed after all.

Thank goodness I leave tomorrow. When I return from my trip to attend Reggie's wedding, I will figure out how to move out of this hole. I can't stay here much longer.

When I wake up the next morning, my head is foggy from the weed blown in my face. But remembering what day it is, I squeal and kick my legs under the sheet on my bed because in a few hours I'll see my best friend and I can't wait. Everything is packed and loaded into my car, and when I lock the front door, I can hardly contain my excitement. At the airport, the lines to pass through security are a joke. I barely have time to board the plane before they close the gate.

The airplane smells like sweat and dirty carpet, not great scents to have to deal with for the next two and a half hours. Though in some respects, it's better than the weed from next door. I am definitely not going to miss that over the next ten days.

My BFF, Reggie, is getting hitched, and since I'm the maid of honor, I plan on living it up with her during her last days as a single lady. According to her, a group of us will be going dancing tonight, which loosely translates to couples plus Stacey. This should be interesting.

I mean fun. Tonight will be fun.

Staring out at the tarmac, my elbow is suddenly knocked from the armrest, making me toss my phone to the floor. "Shit," I say, trying to lean forward in the cramped space to find it. Stretching awkwardly between the wall of the plane and the seat in front of me, my fingers finally wrap around my cell. Sitting up quickly, the back of my head smacks into something hard. Rubbing the sore spot with my free hand, I turn to the person trying to kill me.

"Sorry," he says, slowly reaching his fingers toward my head. Um, hello, tall, not so dark, and handsome. The guy is wearing a pair of trendy jean shorts and a thick white t-shirt which shows off his muscular, corded arms and the intricate tattoo on his left bicep that stops right above his elbow. His icy blue eyes search mine and my mouth goes dry. His dark blond hair is longer on top and shaved close to his scalp on the sides. A thick, neatly trimmed beard lines his face.

"You okay?" he asks, leaning closer, allowing me to catch his scent of citrus, rosemary, and musk.

Pasting on a smile, because ouch, but *hello, gorgeous*, I say, "I'm good. How's your elbow?"

Man Candy grins, though it fades quickly and never meets his eyes. There's a depth to them, unlike anything I've ever seen. He carries something inside, tucked deep down, but that kind of sadness still seeps through eyes like his, like pale blue glass.

"Elbow's good," he answers, sitting in the seat next to me. This plane isn't big, it has three seats on one side and two seats on the other, and when I booked the flight his seat was empty. Now he fills it—completely. His long legs barely fit in front of him, so his knees are bent, hips open wide, making it impossible for any personal space. My eyes travel down the length of his body and stop on his tanned and toned legs with the dusting of dark blond hairs. I'm wearing jeans, but I can still feel the heat of his skin through the dark denim and it rushes through me like a gust of wind racing through my veins.

"This okay? My leg here?" he asks, forcing my gaze back to his eyes. I flash a tight grin and nod my head. Rather enthusiastically, unfortunately. "I'm Ace." His hand crosses the chair arm, reaching for mine. Shaking hands is a dying art, and when done in the small confines of an airplane it's awkward. But I'm not one to deny myself the pleasures of a touch from a good-looking man. My hand reaches his and it dwarfs mine. Ace's grip is firm, warm, and when he doesn't release his grasp, I start to pull away but stop when his thumb moves over the back of my hand.

When the skin of his knee touches my jeans it sends a pulse of heat zipping through me. And the graze of his thumb on my skin is like multiple lightning strikes. My entire body is on fire.

"Stacey," I say, clearing my throat, trying to fight the heat rising to my cheeks. I'm a redhead so when I blush, I blush everywhere.

Ace slides his hand from mine, pulls out his phone, and unlocks it. Just when I think he's going to ask for my number—which I wouldn't have given him...*probably*—he switches it to airplane mode.

"Nice to meet you, Stacey."

"Yeah, you too." For the next two and a half hours we banter back and forth until the plane lands in Warner, Washington. I'm eager to meet up with Reggie and give her one heck of a hug since it feels like we haven't seen each other in years. In reality, it's only been a little over a month since I watched her, Jordan, and their son, Micah, drive away. I cried. A lot.

As Ace and I walk up the jetway, it occurs to me that since he lives here, maybe he'd like to meet up later and go dancing. I've enjoyed his company and I could use the moral support since I'm the only single one going out tonight.

"Hey," I say, stopping in the middle of the tunnel. "A group of us are going dancing later at some place called Club Beach. You wanna meet up?"

Ace's lips part and then quirk to one side. His icy blue eyes drill into me, making my body flush with heat. I left the scorching temperatures in Phoenix only to come to Warner and practically get a heat rash from this guy. We separate, letting other passengers through the jetway.

"Wouldn't that be weird?" he asks, pulling his phone from the shorts pocket over his thigh.

"Um, no." I laugh awkwardly, feeling the heat climbing up my neck. *Calm the spaz, Stace.* "The only weird thing about tonight is the fact I'm going out with my best friend, her fiancé, and another couple. I'm the single one...hello, awkward."

"So, it's a couples thing?"

I shrug, letting a few more people by and then

start walking toward the gate. It was just a thought; maybe it would have saved me from feeling like the third wheel. Scratch that—fifth wheel. But he's not into it, no biggie.

"Hey, wait up," he says, wrapping his large hand around my elbow, turning me to face him. "I didn't say no."

"You didn't say yes either." Gently, I pull my arm from his grasp and plaster on a fake smile. "It was nice to meet you, Ace." My purse slips down over my shoulder, so I return the strap and then rush out of the jetway into the terminal gate. Finding the signs for baggage claim, I make my way through the airport but stop at the restroom first. On my way out of the bathroom, I run—forehead first—into a firm chest covered in a thick white t-shirt that smells like citrus, rosemary, and musk.

Ace's hands grip my arms to steady me, but really all they do is make my knees weak from the way my body reacts to his touch. What the freak?

"What time do I need to show up tonight?" he asks, running his gaze over my face, pausing at my lips before quickly returning to my eyes.

"I'm not desperate." I shake out of his grasp and step back. "Don't feel like you *need* to show up to put me out of my misery. I don't *need* you to go."

"Okay, let me rephrase that." A muscle in his jaw ticks before he continues. "I would love to meet up later. What time and where can I pick you up?"

"It's not a date," I say, smiling and ducking my chin toward my chest.

"Are you going to let me take you out or not?" he asks, laughing and closing the small distance between us. His head drops level with mine, and his eyes drill into me. Ace brings his hand to my wrist and settles his fingers over my racing pulse.

I inhale sharply at how this touch feels so intimate, how it takes my wildly beating heart and makes the blood rocket through my veins. I seriously need to rein in these crazy hormones. Because that's all this is—overactive, lust-filled hormones that will only end in disappointment.

"We're all staying the night at the Parkview Inn. Do you know where that is?" I ask, unable to stop the heat creeping up my neck. He nods, offering me another grin that doesn't reach his eyes. "Pick me up at eight?"

"Eight, got it," he says, unlocking his phone. "What's your number?"

I shake my head. "I'll just meet you in the lobby."

"All right." Ace drops my wrist, winks, and walks away. This should be interesting telling Reggie I've got a date.

Once I pass by security, I see Reggie and Micah waiting for me and my heart swells. Space is what I wanted when I moved out of the apartment we shared for nine years, and space is what I got. Never would have guessed it would be a distance of fifteen hundred miles, though.

Micah runs to me, wraps his arms around my waist, and squeezes me tight. Reggie joins our hug and relief washes over me that I'm finally here. My best friend is getting married and I couldn't be happier for her.

Acknowledgements

Wow! What amazing support I've received from readers since releasing my first book, *Raining Down Rules* in February. Because of you, book three in the *Raining Down Series* was written and is slated for an early 2017 release. So, thank you! Thank you for reading Jemma, Jordan, and Vic's story and asking for more. I sincerely hope you loved Jordan's story of finding love in *Raining Down Redemption*. His was a story I couldn't wait to tell.

To my beta readers, Michelle, Colleen, and Kaitlyn—you ladies are amazing and I can't thank you enough for your feedback, advice, and encouragement. You all are rock stars!

To K. Johnson Editorial—Oh. My. Goodness. You are amazing at what you do and without your ninja editing skills, this book wouldn't be half as good as it is. I really need to figure out how to send you some of my brownies!

Mom and Dad, thank you for supporting me and encouraging me to write what I love. I love you both so much.

To my book club girls—love you all!

Once again, to Bonnie, thank you for the late night chats and word wars. Thank you for encouraging me to keep writing. Thank you for your friendship all these years!

Thank you to Jennifer and Jessica of Limitless Publishing for taking a chance on the Raining Down series. Thank you for making my dream a reality.

And thank you to my editor at Limitless, Gillian. Once again, you've put the polish on this story and I can't tell you how much I appreciate all that you do.

And finally, TOJ Publishing Services, your covers are amazing! Thank you for bringing *Raining Down Redemption* to life.

About the Author

BK Rivers grew up riding through rolling fields of grain on horseback, driving hay trucks and catching frogs in a silver creek.

BK, her husband and three children live in the Phoenix suburbs on their own mini farm surrounded by crowing roosters and the low nicker of horses. When she's not writing, she can be found baking anything sweet, in fact it's been said her brownies are so good they save marriages.

The inspiration for her novels comes in many forms, but mostly from her Gotye channel on Pandora. She writes young adult and new adult novels to the beat of Gotye, Snow Patrol and many others.

Facebook:
http://www.facebook.com/BKRivers.Author

Twitter:
http://twitter.com/WriterRivers

Website:
http://www.BKRivers.com

Sign up for my newsletter to stay up to date on new releases:
http://eepurl.com/bQ525r